BLACK
Beauty

Also by
Constance Burris

Chaos

Coal: Book One of the Everleaf Series

BLACK *Beauty*

CONSTANCE BURRIS

SHEMEYA

A woman who cuts her hair is about to change her life. — Coco Chanel

S hemeya jumped out of the green pleather seat, ignoring the bus driver's grunt of annoyance as he pulled the lever and opened the doors. As soon as she could, she squeezed through the opening and hopped off the crowded bus.

While she walked through the maze of cracked concrete sidewalks, the hot Oklahoma wind thrashed her face and sweat prickled her skin. Vista Apartments, unlike the two apartment complexes flanking it, had green siding that was well maintained and the parking lots only had a few potholes.

"What's wrong with you, girl?"

Surprised, Shemeya stopped. The question had come from Crazy Jade. She'd popped up two years ago out of nowhere. There were a dozen rumors about her circulating through the apartments, including one about her being a voodoo priestess.

Jade stood a few feet away in the open doorway of her apartment. Shemeya's mom would have killed her if she'd done that - flies and air conditioning and money not growing on trees and all. Shemeya wanted to keep walking, but she didn't want to be rude. Jade was the only parent who didn't pay for babysitting with food stamps.

"Why are you in such a hurry?" Jade asked. With her light skin and brown freckles, she didn't look anything like her dark-skinned five-year-old son, Coal, who stood nearby bouncing a basketball.

"I have homework to do," Shemeya lied, trying to focus her attention on Jade instead of the three girls walking from the bus stop. Latreece, Benita, and Aaliyah were cousins and protected each other like sisters. If one of the girls hated you, all three hated you. And right now Shemeya was number one on Latreece's crap list.

"Move, Medusa," Latreece said, hitting Shemeya's shoulder as she walked by. As if on cue, Benita and Aaliyah followed suit, almost knocking Shemeya to the ground.

"What's that about?" Jade stepped onto the sidewalk, standing next to Shemeya. "Ad why'd they call you Medusa?"

Shemeya blinked the sun out of her eyes and pulled her shirt away from her moist armpits. "No, reason. Just stupid girls saying stupid things." Medusa had been her nickname after she'd started growing dreads her freshman year. The constant teasing almost made her cut them out.

"Are they the reason you've stopped smiling?"

Shemeya arched an eyebrow. "Stopped smiling . . . What are you talking about?"

"You've always been full of joy. That's why I like it when you watch Coal. He always comes back happy." Jade stepped closer. "But now your smile is gone."

My smile? Shemeya thought. *Who pays attention to someone's smile?*

2

"There's nothing wrong with me."

Jade folded her arms across her chest. "I've been here for two years and I've never seen you sad. Let me help you."

"There's nothing wrong with me and I don't need help."

Shemeya paused and lowered her voice. "So is it true, though? Are you a voodoo priestess?"

Jade laughed. Her eyes sparkled for a moment and seemed to turn from muddy brown to red. "I don't know nothing about voodoo, child," she said in a mocking, thick Cajun accent. "But I do admire their results."

Shemeya twirled a dread around her finger. "Anyways, I don't have any money."

"I don't need your money. You are one of the only people in Vista Apartments who dares to smile." Jade placed a hand on Shemeya's shoulder. "Let me help."

She stepped away from Jade's touch. "This conversation is getting too weird, Ms. Jade. I have to go. Call me this weekend if you need a babysitter."

Shaking her head, Shemeya turned to Coal. "Bye, Cutie."

Good luck on having a normal life with that weird-ass mom of yours.

She walked the rest of the way to her apartment and up the concrete stairs. She forced herself not to look down, but once she got to the door, she couldn't help it. Jade stared at her from below. From this angle, the sun beamed on Jade's face and her muddy brown eyes appeared to glow red.

Shemeya stood in the hallway eating a bowl of cereal. Iris, her younger sister, squirmed as their mother ran a comb through the girl's kinky hair. The medicated scent of Blue

Magic hair grease mingled oddly with the sweet smell of Frosted Flakes. The good thing about dreads: she never had to get another scalp burn from a relaxer and she never had to comb her hair.

"Momma, since you don't work today can you take me to school? The bus has been late for the past three days." Shemeya had spent part of the morning practicing how to ask the question so it sounded casual, instead of like the desperate plea for help it was.

"Hell, no." Mary pulled the comb roughly through Iris's hair before she pointed it at Shemeya. "And if you miss that bus I'm gonna whoop your ass. I don't care if you are about to graduate. You ain't too old to get a beating."

"You could have just said no," Shemeya muttered.

"What did you say?"

Mary worked as a health care worker and traveled from house to house, cleaning crap and cooking crap, as she put it. When she got home, she'd always tell them, "I deal with too much crap at work to hear it from my kids."

"Nothing. Bye," Shemeya said hurriedly, placing the empty bowl on the kitchen counter. She grabbed her backpack and raced out of the apartment before her mother could deliver any more threats involving someone's ass getting beat.

She had known the chances of her mother taking her to school were slim so she headed out of the apartments and walked the three blocks to stand in line for the neighborhood bus.

The apartment kids were not allowed to ride the neighborhood's bus, and the neighborhood kids were not

4

allowed to ride the apartment's bus. Separating them had been the school's half-assed attempt at keeping the well-off bougie kids from the poorer kids, but the yuppie kids had moved out of this area years ago. Everyone in this part of town either received welfare benefits or they were one paycheck away from living on the streets.

Once the neighborhood bus arrived, she lowered her head and followed the other students. She chose a seat in the middle of the bus away from the driver's line of sight. While she removed her backpack, she noticed a few stares, but no one said anything.

When the bus started moving, she closed her eyes and let out a sigh of relief.

"What are you doing on my bus?"

She swallowed the lump in her throat and looked up. Jason, her chemistry partner, stood in the aisle.

"It's a free world. I can ride this bus if I want to."

He sat down, put his arm around the back of the seat, and leaned towards her. He was so close she saw flecks of dry skin on his forehead. Jason's hair was shaved close at the sides, and his perfectly coifed box rose half a foot above his head. Jason and another guy, Andre, were in competition for who could grow the biggest box. Unfortunately, Jason was winning. "No, you can't. No Vista kids are allowed on this bus."

Shemeya scowled. "You gonna tell on me?"

Jason laughed. "No, I wouldn't do that to you. Anyway, our chemistry project is due soon. You want to meet up at my place today and work on it?"

"Sure." She took a deep breath. "I thought you were gonna snitch, and then I was gonna have to cut you."

He grabbed her arm and laughed, letting his hand linger. "Do you know I wouldn't do you like that. So why are you on this bus?"

She turned from him and slipped lower into the seat. "No, reason. I just wanted to change it up."

The twenty-minute ride through the outskirts of south west Oklahoma City took Shemeya past cow pastures and oversized warehouses. According to her sophomore history teacher, the Gene Autry school district was created to fight the desegregation of public schools in the 1950s. But forty years later, Blacks, Hispanics, and Vietnamese made up thirty percent of the school district as more minorities moved into the suburbs. As she entered the school, fliers requesting her vote for the next student president and posters daring her to say no to drugs littered the walls.

"Hey, Shemeya." Sam, a fellow senior that hadn't talked to her since freshman year, walked beside her. His grin revealed a mouth full of gold caps. "You want to meet up later?"

"No," she said. "Why would I want to do that? I hardly know you."

"Well, I heard you were down for anything and I wanted to know if you wanted to hook up later."

She stopped. "Who told you that?"

"Everybody knows about what happened between you and Sean. So, what's up? You want to hook up?" he said, grabbing his crotch.

"Eww. No."

Sam seized her hand and placed a piece of paper in her palm. "Here's my number. Call me if you change your mind. I've always wondered what it would be like to pull on those dreads."

Shemeya's mouth fell open and she threw the paper into his face. Before she could curse him out, someone pushed her from behind. Her hands broke her fall as she went crashing to the floor. Embarrassed and uncomfortably aware of everyone in the hallway staring at her, she looked up.

Latreece stood above her, lips pressed and shoulders back. "Watch where you're going, Medusa."

"What's going on?" asked Mrs. Smith, the tenth-grade social studies teacher, who thankfully, had been passing by.

"I'm sorry. That was an accident." Latreece sneered at Shemeya before she turned and blended back into the crowd of students.

Mrs. Smith bent down and helped Shemeya pick up her bag. "Are you okay? I can report her to the office, she glanced down the hallway. "That didn't look like an accident."

"I'm all right." Shemeya forced herself to stop trembling and hurriedly walked in the opposite direction of Latreece and her first-hour class.

She managed to avoid Latreece for the rest of the day, but she had been tripped, jabbed, and propositioned by half of the school.

Through all of the taunting, she'd kept her head high and her face straight. But the quiet walk through her apartment complex destroyed the flimsy barrier she'd built during school. Tears streamed uncontrollably down her cheeks. She tried to wipe them away, but more quickly took their place.

As she turned towards her apartment, she kept her head low, hoping no one would see her crying. She lifted her head to gauge her location and noticed Jade. The woman stood in the same spot as yesterday, staring at Shemeya intensely.

She stopped and wiped her face with her shirt sleeve. "How can you help me?"

A slow grin crept across Jade's face.

She followed Jade through the living room, past Coal asleep on the couch, and into the master bedroom. All of the three-bedroom apartments were the same. This would have been her mother's room, but there was no bed, and plants were everywhere. Dozens of plants: potted plants, hanging plants, creeping plants. Even though she'd taken botany for two years, Shemeya couldn't name any of them.

Two windows filled the east side of the room, but hundreds of vines had crept up the wall, and in their greed, had blocked most of the sunlight.

"What is all of this?" Shemeya asked. The moisture in the air clung to her skin and sank into her chest, making it hard to breathe.

"These are my other babies," Jade said in the same affectionate tone she used when she spoke about her son. She walked through the labyrinth of plants and stopped at a table on the far side of the room, barely visible through the foliage. On it lay a pestle and mortar, and inside the mortar Shemeya saw something amazingly similar to . . .

"Is that weed?" Shemeya gasped. "You grow pot?" She looked towards the door expecting to see the police. The last thing she needed was to get caught in a drug dealer's house.

Jade laughed as she pulled a leaf from a plant with green and purple leaves. "This is much better than weed. It's from my homeland. And, most importantly, it's not illegal here."

"Oh," Shemeya said, a little disappointed. She hadn't wanted to get caught with a drug dealer, but she wasn't opposed to smoking a little bit of weed though.

"Where are you from?" Shemeya asked.

"No place you've heard of."

"I'm not stupid. I got an A in geography-- Ow." Shemeya shrieked in response to Jade yanking one of her locs. "You almost pulled out a dread."

"For it to work for *you*, it needs a bit of *you* in it." Jade held the hair in front of her face. "These five strands should be enough." She placed them into the mortar and started grinding it into the marble bowl with the leaves.

Shemeya rubbed her head while she watched the hair became indistinguishable from the other ingredients. "Is this voodoo?"

"No. This isn't voodoo." Jade ground the mixture faster, causing the pestle to clang loudly against the marble bowl.

"Then what is it? My mom would kill me if she knew I was messing around with voodoo."

"It's an herbal medicine. When you receive blood, the doctors have to make sure they match your blood type, right?

Well, adding your hair makes the herbs specific for you. Like recognizes like."

"But what does it do? Will it get me high?"

"It will give you courage and confidence, but it will not get you high."

Disappointed, Shemeya watched Jade roll the herbs inside a small sheet of paper. "It looks just like a joint to me."

"It is not a joint," Jade said sharply, handing it to Shemeya. "Smoke it here so I know I haven't wasted my time."

Shemeya studied the fake joint. She should have walked right past this place and left Crazy Jade to her craziness. But after the day she'd endured, she couldn't tolerate the thought of going back to school. Maybe, just maybe, smoking this would make it all go way. Besides, what would some herbs hurt?

"Okay." Shemeya placed the tip of the faux joint into her mouth, and Jade lit it.

Shemeya inhaled. The smoke traveled through her mouth, down her throat, and settled in her lungs for a few intense moments before Shemeya exhaled. "Dang, that's nasty." But the taste didn't stop her from bringing it back to her lips and inhaling once again.

Shemeya knocked on Jason's door. For the past three years, they'd ended up in the same chemistry course as lab partners. He'd asked her out a few times, but she'd politely said no. He was smart and decent looking, but he bored her. Turning him down made her feel like an idiot who only dated thugs, but she wasn't stupid. She only wanted a little thug, not a full serving.

When Jason answered the door, she pulled off her backpack and stepped into the house. "Is your mom home?"

"No, she's with her new guy," he said, leading her into his kitchen. "Want something to drink?"

"You got some juice?" Shemeya desperately wanted to wash away the dry, earthy taste the herbs had left in her mouth. Water hadn't worked.

"I got something better." He reached under one of the kitchen cabinets and pulled out a bottle of Hennessey.

"Jason, really?" She cocked her head to the side, and he smiled innocently.

She rolled her eyes. "Sure. I need a drink after the day I've had." *And liquor should kill the taste in my mouth.*

He poured the cognac into two yellow Solo plastic cups, before they walked into the living room and sat on the couch.

She only took a small sip but it was enough to warm her from the inside out and sear away the taste of the herbs.

"We should be talking about absorption, not sitting here getting drunk," Shemeya pointed out, sitting the cup on the living room table.

"We always finish our projects tipsy. Why should this time be any different?"

Shemeya laughed, remembering all of the late night homework sessions they'd had in the past. They didn't talk much in school, but she enjoyed hanging out with him. He was funny and thoughtful when he didn't have a group of other people around him. "Anyways, let's get started:

absorption vs. adsorption." She pulled her chemistry book from her bag.

"Stupid names. Why do they have to be so similar?" He sat back on the couch with a glazed look in his eyes.

"Are you going to get your books?"

He licked his lips and leaned forward. "I've heard stories about you and Latreece's boyfriend."

"So?" The small buzz she had from the liquor quickly dissipated while her heart raced. She dreaded where the conversation was headed.

"I don't understand. I've been asking you out for months, but you go out with him instead. He has a girlfriend."

"I didn't go out with him," she said through clenched teeth. She'd expected to be harassed at school; she hadn't expected it here. She had hoped her anger would shut him up, but no such luck.

"I saw you go in the room with Sean last weekend at Serena's party."

She threw her books on the table and stood. "Jason. Really?"

"I've treated you with nothing but respect since I've known you."

"I've had a horrible day with everyone teasing me at school. I get here and have to deal with it from you, too. Forget you. I'm leaving." She turned from him and bent over to pick up her books.

"Are you crying?"

She brought her hand up to her face, it came back wet. Why was she crying in front of him? Wasn't the fake weed supposed to give her courage?

"Don't go. I'm sorry."

She was so busy wiping away her tears that she didn't fight it when he grabbed her hand and pulled her back onto the couch. "I'm sorry. I shouldn't have said anything."

She let him hold her as she cried. Maybe it was the liquor, maybe it was the fake weed, or maybe it was her loneliness, but whatever the reason she didn't stop him when he brought his lips down onto hers.

His sweaty hands on her breast brought her back to reality. He wasn't who she wanted. "No, Jason." She pulled back. "I have to go."

"Don't go," he pleaded, with his hand still under her shirt.

Somehow they'd ended up on the couch with him on top and straddled between her legs.

"No." She tried to move from under him.

He loomed above her, flushed despite his dark skin. "Do you like it rough? Is that what it is?"

"No. This isn't what I came here for." When pushing didn't move him, Shemeya punched his shoulders and chest, but he refused to budge.

He kissed her neck. "I'm tired of being the nice guy," he whispered in her ear, pinning her further beneath his body.

"Get off me!" she screamed. His erection rubbed against the crotch of her jeans. She punched at his back and, but it only made him more excited. Her scalp itched as she fought. She wanted to scratch it, but she needed both hands to fight

13

Jason. *I'm getting raped, but I can't resist the urge to scratch.* The inconvenience of it almost made her laugh.

Something above moved. She looked past Jason. Five snakes hovered above his head.

"I'm going crazy," she thought. This time she did laugh, and the snakes, which were the same rusty brown color as her dreads, returned her smile.

The itching had been replaced with pleasurable tingles that ran from her head down to her toes.

He must have sensed a change, because Jason paused and looked towards her. "Why are you laughing?" His gaze darted above her head. The feel of his erection disappeared as he moved away, but she wrapped her legs around his waist.

"Where are you going?" Shemeya asked.

"We need to leave," he said, trembling. "There are snakes in here. There are snakes in your hair." She pulled him closer while he fought to be released. "Let go. We need to get out of here!"

"No, stay," she whispered in his ear. "They won't hurt you."

Shaking and wide-eyed, he looked from Shemeya to the snakes. He tried to move away. This time when she attempted to pull him closer, he punched her. Pain exploded in her jaw, but she didn't let go.

"Jason, that hurt."

He looked into her eyes. "Please," he begged just as a snake sunk its fangs into his cheek. Another struck his ear. One clung to his nose. And another hung below his left eye. He screamed and writhed in pain as he tried to escape the snakes and Shemeya's thighs. His pleading dark-brown eyes focused on her before finally, he stopped moving altogether. The snakes retracted their fangs. She relaxed her legs. And Jason fell onto the carpeted floor.

She stood and nearly fainted before she righted herself by grabbing the side of the couch. She brought her hands up to fix her hair but hesitated a few inches away. She'd never touched snakes before. But the snakes came to her, caressing her open palm. They were cold, smooth, and full of life.

The next day, Shemeya stared in the bathroom mirror at a large, imposing bruise on her jaw. The blue and purple mark contrasted sharply with her brown skin. While trying to ignore the pain, she brushed her teeth. She had no idea how she got home yesterday. All she remembered was fighting off Jason and having some type of hallucination about snakes. No, the herb didn't get her high, but it sure as hell made her delusional.

Shemeya covered her bruised jaw with foundation before she braided her dreads in an intricate twist that fell down her back. *I look good*, she thought as she admired herself in the mirror.

Her mom popped her head into the bathroom. "I'm passing your school on the way to a patient's house, you want a ride?"

"Yes!" Shemeya exclaimed, relieved she wouldn't have to see Jason or Latreece on either bus.

"Hurry up. I'm leaving in five minutes."

Shemeya appreciated herself in the mirror one last time before she walked out.

As she pulled in front of the school, Mary turned in her seat, "I want to talk to you." Her usual confidence wavered a bit, which told Shemeya she wouldn't like what her mother was about to say.

"What's wrong?" Shemeya asked.

"I've been hearing stories about Jade messing in voodoo, witchcraft, and miracle cures. I don't know what's going on, but I don't want you going near her."

Too late for that. Shemeya thought. "She's crazy, but Coal is pretty normal."

"Stay away from Jade," her mom reiterated, "and Coal."

Shemeya lifted an eyebrow and let out a deep breath. "Okay." That wouldn't be a problem after she had me smoke those crazy herbs.

"Well, good," Mary said, sounding as if she had been expecting a bigger fight.

"By the way, you look pretty," Mary said as Shemeya opened her car door and stepped out. "Those dreads are looking nice."

Shemeya furrowed her brow and touched her hair. *No snakes.* "Thank you."

"Maybe I'll grow me some. I'm tired of messin' with those damn relaxers."

As Mary drove away, Shemeya stood in front of the school gaping. Her mother had never complimented her dreads. Never.

Shemeya sat in her third-hour chemistry class, pretending to study the course notes from yesterday. No one had pushed, groped, or called her names. Her mother, who had never approved of her hair, had even given her a compliment. She'd been taught dreads were unnatural and dirty. But once started, they naturally locked on their own. And, unlike when she had a relaxer, she could wash them as much as she wanted without messing it up.

She gnawed on her pencil and smiled. Maybe the herbs had worked. She felt strong, confident and beautiful. Now, if she could only get out of seeing Jason. His seat was empty. Maybe he'd skip today and save both of them the embarrassment of having to deal with what happened last night. She could barely remember any of it, but the throbbing in her jaw wasn't reassuring.

"I'm sorry to hear about your lab partner." Jasmine, an advanced placement sophomore, stood beside Shemeya's lab table. She grinned then quickly frowned, as if she remembered that what she was about to say was bad news

"What are you talking about?" Shemeya asked, staring up at Jasmine's shiny metal braces.

"He was sent to the hospital last night from not one but five snake bites." She stopped for a breath and licked her braces. "They were poisonous, and the doctors aren't sure if he'll live. If it were just one or two bites, maybe he'd be okay, but I don't see how anyone one can survive five snake bites."

Shemeya's chest tightened. "How do you know this?"

"It was on the news. They didn't release his name, but I live down the street from him. I saw the ambulance and the news trucks last night at his house."

Damn! Shameya's eyes widened and her mouth fell open as she remembered the hallucination from last night. Without another word, Shemeya stood, pushed past Jasmine and ran out of the classroom and into the girl's bathroom. She took down her braid and ran her fingers through her dreads and along her scalp.

Nothing lived in her hair.

Her dreads were not alive.

Whatever had happened to Jason had nothing to do with her.

Nothing.

Relieved and thoroughly convinced she possessed dreads instead of snakes, Shemeya stepped into the hallway. However, her relief was short lived.

Latreece stood outside the bathroom. She looked like she was skipping volleyball practice because she wore a pair of too short, too-tight gym shorts that highlighted her tall skinny legs. Her cousins and a small group of students wearing the same gym uniform surrounded her.

Latreece separated herself from the crowd. "I've been looking for you."

Damn Latreece and her grudges! Shemeya looked for an escape. She needed a way to leave without looking like a punk. "I'm not in the mood to deal with you right now, Latreece." Shemeya tried to push Latreece to the side, but she grabbed Shemeya's arm and pulled her back.

"No, we're dealing with this now." Latreece swung her fist and hit Shemeya in the eye.

Shemeya fell to the floor. Flashes of light exploded across her closed eyelids. She had no idea that bag of bones could hit so hard. Before she could recover, Latreece hopped on top of her and began pummeling Shemeya's face.

Shemeya's scalp started to itch.

The same itch she'd had when she'd been fighting Jason. *Damn, it hadn't been a hallucination!* The itching increased, eclipsing the pain from Latreece's punches. She needed to get out of there before the entire school saw her.

Taking a deep breath, she used her body weight to roll over. Latreece tumbled to the ground. Shemeya hurried to her feet and she ran through the crowd and down the hallway as fast as she could.

The snakes hissed as she rushed away, sending tingles through her body. Desperate, she ran into to an empty classroom, switched off the lights, and hid in a closet at the back of the room. Everything had been fine up until that bitch had attacked her. Mind racing, she realized the same thing had happened with Jason. She was fine until he tried to rape her. The snakes must be connected with her anger.

If she calmed down, would they go away? She sat stooped in the corner of the closet and caressed her hair, hoping it would calm them, calm her.

The door to the classroom opened. Her stomach lurched, and the snakes began to move again.

No, she thought, panicked. She needed to stay calm. Whoever it is would go away.

"Shemeya?" said a voice from inside of the room.

Damn, it was Sean, Latreece's boyfriend. But he'd also been Shemeya's first love. She'd broken up with him during freshman year to date a senior. She learned too late the older boy had only wanted one thing. When he got it, he never talked to her again.

"Please go away," she shouted. Suspecting he wouldn't, Shemeya re-braided her hair, and hid the snakes in the braid as best she could. Just as she'd finished, the closet light switched on.

"Shemeya, are you okay?" Sean stepped into the closet and kneeled so that they were face-to-face. "I'm sorry about Latreece."

The concern in his eyes melted her heart. "How can you stand to be with someone like that?"

"She's not usually like that. She's been acting crazy since the party last week."

"If you didn't want to piss her off, then why did you tell the entire school we slept together?" Shemeya asked, louder than she intended.

"I didn't tell anyone we slept together."

"Then why all the stories? Everyone thinks I'm a ho, and your girlfriend just kicked my ass."

"An entire room of people saw you pull me into that room at the party."

He stood. She grabbed his hand and allowed him to pull her onto her feet. "You could have told everyone the truth," Shemeya said.

"I did. No one believed me." When they had dated, he was awkward and gawky, but over the past few years, he'd turned into one of the finest boys in school. She shouldn't have broken up with him. He had been the one to encourage her to grow dreads after her hair had broken off from a bad relaxer.

"Why didn't anything happen at the party?" Shemeya asked. "You wanted to at first."

He looked away, but not before I saw regret in his eyes. "That was a mistake. I'm with Latreece. I shouldn't have let it get that far." He tried to walk towards the closet door, but she moved in front of him, placing her hands on his chest.

"Please don't go." Just touching him sent pleasurable chills down her spine.

"I only came to make sure you were okay." He met her gaze. "You look fine, so I need to go. Latreece will kill me if she catches me in here."

Shemeya grabbed his shirt. "No one will see us this time." He tried harder to move past her but he stopped suddenly, his entire body rigid underneath her hands.

"Why does it look like there are snakes in your hair?" he asked, taking slow tentative steps backwards.

"Don't worry about them. If you are nice to me, they'll be nice to you." She should have been worried, but his presence made her giddy and light headed. The snakes liked him and she needed to tell him how she felt. "I miss you."

He gasped and covered his mouth with a trembling hand. Sean gaped at the snakes. "You been messing with Crazy Jade, haven't you?"

She shrugged and let go of his shirt. "Maybe."

"Shemeya, there are snakes attached to your head. That ain't normal."

"Why aren't you surprised?" She patted her hair, and the snakes moved to stroke her hand.

"Crazy things like this always happened in New York."

21

She grimaced, not understanding what he said. "It's common to have dreadlocked snakes there?"

"No, but there are so many damn fairies coming through, anything's possible." Sean's voice shook with apprehension and fear.

"Fairies? Like gay people?" Shemeya asked. She'd never seen him so scared. For a second, she wondered if he might be going crazy, but the entire situation was crazy.

"No, fairies like monsters." Sean took another step back and nervously rubbed a hand over his head. "Oh, damn! Did you attack Jason?"

She bit her lip, suppressing the urge to cry. How did such a great day end up so bad? "I didn't hurt him. The snakes did, and I didn't know my hair was going to turn into snakes, and I didn't know Jason would try to rape me. The snakes were only trying to protect me."

"Calm down, Shemeya." He grabbed her shoulders, preventing her from moving and forcing Shemeya to look up to meet his gaze. His top lip was twisted in disgust. "You need to get rid of those snakes before anyone finds out."

"So you won't tell anyone about Jason?"

"It was an accident and won't nobody believe me anyway."

"Do you think Jade will take the snakes away?"

"No. Don't go near her." He pulled Shameya out of the closet and into the classroom.

"Just cut them off," he said, pulling out a pair scissors from the teacher's desk.

"You gotta be kidding! I've been growing these for four years."

"Your dreads turn into snakes. If you don't have the dreads, then you don't have snakes."

Both she and the snakes cringed as Sean held out the ominous metallic scissors.

Her dreads were a part of her. They separated her from everyone else. She ran her fingers through her hair and the snakes. The decision should have been simple: dreads or a normal life. So why was she hesitating to choose?

ASHLEY

I think that the most important thing a woman can have- next to talent, of course- is her hairdresser. — Joan Crawford

shley's face contorted in pain, and her eyes teared while a wide-tooth comb traveled through her thick, dry, coiled hair.

"You're the only mixed girl I know with hair worse than regular black folks," Chantel said, sucking on her teeth. Chantel was skinny, had a medium brown complexion, and she wore a gold hooped nose ring.

"Damn you, Chantal. Why do you have to say that every time you do my hair?" Ashley's white father should have guaranteed she'd be born with long curly hair, but instead, she had hair like a wired brillo pad.

When Chantel popped another nap, Ashley screamed and pulled away. Three kids: two girls and a boy between the ages of five and eight, sat on the couch near the shop's window laughing at her pain. She shot them a murderous stare before they looked away, but their giggling only increased. She hated when folks brought their bad ass kids to the salon. They were loud and always made fun of her while she got her hair done.

The 23rd St. Beauty Parlor sat in an old shopping center between a Dollar Store and a bingo hall. Dingy beige paint peeled from the corners of the walls, and strands of black Silky Number 5 littered the floor. One of the three hooded hair dryers sitting in the back of the shop had an out of order sign on the broken plastic seat.

"I need the good stuff," Ashley said, trying to ignore the muffled laughter of the kids.

"The stuff I used last time was the good stuff," Chantel said.

"You know what I mean." Ashley didn't bother to mask her frustration.

"That stuff is illegal."

"Is there anyway you can get your hands on some?" Ashley's hair grew uncontrollably. Until Chantel discovered a product called the Brazilian Blowout, it had never stayed straight for more than a few weeks. The process was banned recently, forcing Ashley to use methods that didn't work nearly as well.

"It's banned for a reason. It has crazy levels of formaldehyde in it." Chantel hit the back of Ashley's chair. "And damn you for not being concerned about my well-being."

"We've been using it for years and neither one of us has ever gotten sick."

"Well, I don't want any problems either." Chantel rolled her eyes and waved the comb back and forth. "I'm not willing to die just 'cause you want your hair straight."

"Just get some weave," said Treva, a short brown-skinned hairstylist, whose workstation sat across from Chantel. From the mirror, Ashley saw Treva gluing black silky tracks of weave onto her client's scalp.

"My man does not like weave." Ashley released a long, sigh and leaned back in the chair. She looked past Chantal and her nose ring to the piss colored stains on the ceiling.

"You know who does use that stuff still?" Treva asked.

"Who?" Ashley shot straight up. The momentum almost sent her out of the chair.

Treva looked above Ashley's head, suddenly silent.

She followed Treva's gaze to see Chantal shaking her head and mouthing the word "no." Ashley turned back to Treva. "Don't listen to her. Who does it?"

"Crazy Jade," Treva said, enunciating each word as if saying the person's name invited something evil and forbidden into the salon.

Ashley furrowed her brow. "Who is Crazy Jade?"

Chantel pointed her comb at Treva. "Really, Treva, really? You just had to say something, didn't you?"

Treva shrugged. "If you ain't gonna straighten it, somebody needs to. Her hair is the nappiest of all nappyville."

The insult hurt, but Ashley boxed the pain away with all of the other hurtful jokes about her nappy hair and sat straighter. "Who is Crazy Jade?"

"That red-headed lady living in your mom's apartment building."

Ashley leaned forward. "You gotta be more specific than that."

"You'd know her if you'd seen her, she's light-skinned and red-headed with freckles."

"Red-headed with freckles? Is she even black?" Ashley asked.

"Her nappy hair makes her black, just like your nappy hair makes you black."

Ashley placed another hurt feeling in her box and transfixed her gaze on Treva. "Is she licensed?"

"Am I licensed?" Treva laughed, dimples appearing on each cheek. "Are any of us licensed?" Ashley looked at the expired certificates on the wall both Chantel and Treva displayed proudly next to their booth.

"Yeah, you got a point," Ashley said, and they all laughed.

After the laughter ended, Treva said, "You can't tell by her nappy hair, but Crazy Jade can do a mean blowout."

"But why do they call her crazy?" Ashley asked.

Treva shrugged, suddenly deciding to pay attention to her client's weave.

Ashley looked at Chantel.

"Don't ask me I don't deal with her. And I ain't gonna curse myself by talking about her."

"Curse? What the hell are you talking about?" Ashley asked. They had given her hope, and now they were taking it away.

"Well, there are different stories," Treva said.

As she spoke, the entire beauty shop quieted. The kids even stopped fighting with each other and crept closer to listen.

"Well, I heard she's a voodoo priestess, and she got run out of Louisiana after they lynched her husband. And," Treva paused and looked around the salon before she stopped at Ashley, "her red hair and red freckles are the marks of the devil."

"That stuff only exists in movies," Ashley said, relieved. Once upon a time she believed those stories, but she'd said 'Bloody Mary' and 'Candy Man' in the mirror enough times to know none of that crap actually existed. "Chantel, what do you think?"

"I think no matter how nappy my hair was, I wouldn't go to her." Chantel lowered her voice and looked towards the kids. "Because from what I hear, she's a witch, and she has a room full of plants and spell books she uses to make her potions that will turn loud-ass nosy-ass kids into roaches." Chantal stomped her foot and the kids (and Ashley and Treva) jumped. "Sit y'all asses down and stay out of grown folk's business."

The trio groaned and skulked back to the couch.

"I don't believe in none of that," Ashley said. "There is no such thing as voodoo priestesses or witches. Treva, you got her number?"

"Nah, she's a competitor, and she's crazy. Why would I have her number? I'm surprised you ain't seen her, though. She always out there at dusk, gossiping just like every other grown ass person in your momma's ghetto apartments."

"Well, Chantel." Ashley hopped off the chair and grabbed a ponytail holder from the counter. "I'm going to see what Crazy Jade can do for me since you're not willing to give me what I want."

"Whatever." Chantel turned towards her mirror, reorganizing the bottles of hair spray and styling gel.

"Don't worry." Ashley pulled her hair into a low ponytail. "I'll be back for my trims and touch-ups."

"You better," Chantel said without turning, but Ashley heard the sparkle in her voice, signifying all was forgiven.

Ashley's mother's apartment sat across from the rental office, the pool, basketball courts, and the playground. Kids were already out sliding down the yellow plastic slides. Occasionally, bursts of laughter were interrupted with angry shouts as two boys, fought over the only working swing. Two groups of giggling girls watched from the shade as teenage boys and a few men ran back and forth on the basketball court with their shirts off. The sweat on their chests glistened in the noonday sun.

This had been the setting of her childhood. Ashley had been raised in various apartments like this, moving every year or two when her mother decided she needed a change or didn't feel like paying the rent.

She missed the busyness of living in apartments. Yeah, everybody knew your business, but drama was preferable to boredom. Two years ago, she'd gotten a government stipend and moved a few miles away into a house in an all-white neighborhood. None of the neighbors talked to each other, and none of the kids were allowed outside to play. The neighborhood was quiet and dull, but her boyfriend, Steven, urged her to stay. The all-white school was better, he'd insisted. Ebony, their daughter, would be guaranteed a better education.

Using her key, Ashley entered her mother's apartment to see Cora and Ebony on the floor playing the Mickey Mouse matching game. From the number of cards on Ebony's side, it looked like Cora was letting the girl win.

"Hi Momma," Ebony said before she turned her attention back to the game and flipped over a card. "I got it, Grandma." She clapped with triumph glittering in her eyes.

If Ebony ever had to choose between Ashley and Cora, her child would choose Cora every time

"Yeah you got it, baby," Cora said with as much joy as Ebony had expressed. Cora had flawless ebony skin and shapely hips and always wore a blonde wig or weave. "You back already?" she asked, leaning onto the living room table to help her stand. "Your hair don't look any better."

Self-consciously, Ashley patted her ponytail. "Chantel doesn't have the stuff I like."

Cora moved to the couch, grabbed a pack of menthol cigarettes and a lighter from the side table. She puffed on the butt of the cigarette as if she'd been waiting for a while to smoke. "That stuff never worked that well anyway." She flicked the cigarette ashes into the ashtray. "You just got nappy hair. But not like my grandbaby. My grandbaby got good hair."

31

At the sound of her name, Ebony looked up, smiled, and returned to her game. She frowned when she saw it wasn't a match.

Ashley bit her lip in frustration. It hurt to see Cora show Ebony so much love when she always took every opportunity to put Ashley down.

"They told me there's a woman in your apartments that can do good blowouts," Chantel said, ignoring the sadness sitting heavy in her chest. "I thought I would go see her."

Cora furrowed her brow. "Who?"

"Crazy Jade," Ashley said, sitting next to Cora.

"She gave me some lightening cream that goes on as smooth as butter. I'm almost as light as you." Cora craned her neck towards Ashley. "See?"

Cora was exaggerating. She was nowhere near light, but she was much lighter. Ashley should have noticed it before, since her face and neck were a good four shades lighter than her chest.

"Maybe I'll go see her right now," Ashley said.

"If she can do hair half as good as she makes bleaching creams, you are gonna have white girl flow. Bet." Cora took a pull of the cigarette and nodded her head, the strands of her blond wig swung from side-to-side.

"But why do they call her crazy?"

"Don't believe what you hear. You know how folks like to gossip. She is just out there trying to make a buck to feed her child. People like to make up stories about her 'cause she don't tell her business."

"Do you know where her apartment is?" Ashley asked.

Cora nodded her head and she inhaled another dose of nicotine. Afterwards, she extinguished the cigarette and opened her front door. She pointed across the complex. "You see that apartment right there?"

"Yeah."

"It's behind that building, on the first floor. It's apartment 180. You can't miss it."

The door to Crazy Jade's apartment stood wide open. A dark-skinned boy sat on the grass near the door playing with a broken tree branch. He was bare-chested and shoeless. His small uneven afro had a twig sticking out of it.

"Hey little man," Ashley said, apprehensively. "Do you live here?"

He looked up and nodded. "Yes." The boy looked to be five-years-old, and he had onyx eyes that didn't seem to have a bottom. Ashley stared at them entranced, trying to decide if his eyes were beautiful or creepy.

Ashley pulled herself from the depth of his gaze, remembering why she'd come. "Does Crazy Jade live here?"

He blinked his long eyelashes. "My momma's name is Jade. She's not crazy, though."

Ashley chuckled. "Oh, sorry. Does Jade live here?"

"Yeah." His short ashy legs were a blur as he ran into the apartment yelling, "Momma!"

A second later, a woman ran out of the back. "What is it?" she shouted, worry and shock flashed in her eyes. She wore a robe that hung halfway open showing her left breast.

Soap bubbles were on her shoulders and neck, water glistened in her red, kinky hair. Her exposed breast and face were covered with mahogany freckles. This was Crazy Jade, Ashley decided. The boy's mother appeared just as they'd said. She had a short, nappy red afro and freckles. She also looked like a boy with a thin frame that barely held an ounce of fat.

"There is someone here for you, Momma," Coal said, still excited.

She looked at Ashley briefly before she returned her attention to Coal. "Coal, all of that screaming scared the hell out of me," she said, shaking his shoulders.

"Sorry, Momma." He stooped his shoulders and shot a nervous glance at Ashley before he turned his gaze to the floor. The duo looked nothing alike. He was as dark as his namesake, but Crazy Jade was as pale as a white lady with the freckles to match. That was the thing with black folks, half the time you never knew what color your kids would be. Chantel had two babies two years apart with the same dad. The girls looked exactly alike, except one had light skin and the other dark.

Jade released Coal and knotted the tie around her robe, finally covering her chest. "What you selling?" she asked, approaching the door.

Ashley noticed white bits of lint clinging to the black robe, and she smelled strawberry body wash. "I heard you could do Brazilian blowouts." Ashley straightened, suddenly aware of the ninety-degree heat, and the sweat beading on her top lip.

"I can," she said.

Ashley's heart leapt. "Do you still use the one with formaldehyde?"

"Coal, go back outside and play," Jade said.

"Excuse me." He ran past Ashley and back outside.

"That product's been banned." Jade crossed her arms in front of her chest.

"I know." Ashley rolled her eyes. "But do you still use it?"

Jade shrugged. "Maybe."

Ashley closed her eyes and silently thanked God. "How much?"

Jade lifted her chin and arched a brow. "You do know it's toxic, right?"

"How much?" Ashley repeated.

"450," Jade said.

"Damn, are you serious?" Two hundred was the most Ashley had ever paid, and she had to practically lie, steal, and cheat to come up with that money.

"Supply and demand," Jade said, tapping her bare foot.

"That's more than twice what I pay at a salon. How about three hundred?" Ashley was desperate, but was she $450 desperate?

"You can't get it at a salon. Four hundred."

"Three-fifty." This time Ashley did not hide the desperation in her voice.

Jade smirked and stepped back from the door. "Are you ready?"

"Yes." Ashley's heart filled with joy as she walked into the apartment. She would have to sell the rest of her food stamps, but straight hair was worth living off ramen noodles and bologna two weeks.

Her enthusiasm was momentarily forgotten when the apartment's humidity hit her in the face.

"Sit here while I go change." Jade pointed to a chair in the kitchen. Ashley walked past the couch, the lone piece of furniture in the living room, and sat at the kitchen table.

Just as Ashley wondered if Crazy Jade was ever coming back, the red-head stepped into the kitchen. She had changed into a pair of loose fitting blue jeans and a black t-shirt.

"Why would you put something so toxic on your hair if you didn't have to?" Jade asked, as she rummaged through the kitchen cabinets.

"It's the only thing that straightens my hair."

Jade pulled out a white container the size of a cereal bowl, an orange rattail comb, and a curling iron from the bottom cabinet. "You're Black, your hair isn't meant to be straight."

"Yeah, but I want good hair." Ashley fidgeted, trying to find a comfortable position in the hard chair. Was she really going to hear a lecture on the harmful effects of Brazilian blowouts and relaxers from someone who straightened hair illegally in her kitchen?

"You mean straight hair?" Jade asked. She placed the container on the table and stood behind Ashley.

"Straight hair or curly hair is good hair. Anything is better than nappy."

Jade undid the ponytail and began pulling her hands through Ashley's coarse hair. She tensed, expecting the woman to pop a nap, but no snap or pain ever came.

Jade opened the container, put on a pair of latex gloves, and began applying the cold cream to Ashley's hair. The smell was a mix between the stench of the last chemistry class she had taken before she'd gotten pregnant and dropped out of school and the flowers at the Myriad Botanical Gardens.

"Why do you think you should have straight hair?" Jade asked, parting Ashley's hair with the tip of the comb.

"Why do you care? You get paid for this. Shouldn't you be encouraging all black women to get their hair straightened?"

"I'm curious. Human psychology has always interested me."

"I'm half white," Ashley said, deciding to tell the truth. "My hair shouldn't be as nappy as it is." It was her hair. She could do whatever she wanted with it.

"Well," Jade said, "I can make your hair so straight you'll never need another Brazilian blowout."

"Really, I won't have any problems with new growth?" Ashley bent her neck so Jade could apply the cream to back of her head.

"No," Jade said. "The product I use reaches into the hair follicle."

"How is that possible?" Ashley mumbled. Her chin was practically touching her chest, and she was having a hard time moving her jaw.

"I've added my own ingredients," Crazy Jade said with pride.

"If you can do that, why don't you straighten your own hair?"

"I had it straightened once, but nappy feels more me than straight." Jade spoke with a confidence Ashley envied.

"I feel more me with straight hair," Ashley said. "Do you think that makes me ashamed of being Black?"

"No, it's just hair. Besides if it made you less Black, then there wouldn't be an authentic Black woman in Oklahoma."

Any response Ashley may have had, was forgotten when two of kids tapped anxiously on Jade's opened door. "What y'all want?" she asked.

"Aunt Effie. Her chest is hurting real bad, and she can't breathe."

"What y'all coming to me for?" Jade asked.

"Cause you're a witch doctor," said a girl with big eyes and two French braids.

"I ain't a witch ..." Jade began but trailed off. "Come on let's go." She removed her gloves, threw them in the trash, and turned to Ashley. "This won't take long. Just in case I'm not back in time, wash that out after ten minutes. Don't leave it in any longer."

"Ten minutes isn't long enough," Ashley said.

"Ten minutes," Jade repeated and followed the kids out of the apartment.

Ashley sat on the chair in the small dining room and tapped her French manicured fingernails on the wooden table stamped with old cup rings and heat stains. The dining room seemed to be an afterthought to the builders. The table and four chairs barely fit into the small space.

She looked at the gold-plated watch on her wrist and exhaled deeply. It felt like an eternity, but only one minute had passed. At the salon, she had Chantel and the other hairstylists to gossip with. Here she didn't even have Crazy Jade since the woman had run off to do God knows what. Why had the kids come to Jade anyway? Was she some type of medicine woman on top of everything else?

She brought her hands to scratch the inevitable burning and tingling that accompanied every Brazilian blowout, but she stopped in midair. Her hair and scalp might be able to take the toxic substance, but she wasn't sure about her unprotected hands. To occupy herself, she started tapping the table again, ignoring the burn. Cora had always told her beauty is pain.

At the two minutes mark, Ashley walked to the cheap fiberboard bookshelf that separated the kitchen from the living room. She trailed an index finger along the children's books on the top and second shelf. Their frayed edges and discolored covers told her they were well read.

She pulled *Where the Sidewalk Ends* by Shel Silverstein from the second shelf. It had been her favorite book as a kid. She loved the goofy pictures and how every other poem was sarcastic, dark, and humorous.

I guess I should start reading to Ebony, Ashley thought as she flipped through the yellowed pages. Maybe if she paid her daughter more attention she'd stopped clinging to Cora so tight.

Five minutes.

As Ashley replaced the poetry book, a book with no title on the spine caught her attention. She picked it up. It had a brown paper bag as its cover. It smelled ancient, and she coughed as the musty smell attacked her sinuses. The paper almost felt handmade. Even if it wasn't, she knew it must be expensive because of the way it bent as she turned every page.

Most of it was written by hand. She couldn't tell if it was written in another language or if it was code, but she could tell they were recipes. Each had what must be a title, a list of ingredients and a paragraph or two below.

She wondered if one of these was the skin whitening cream Cora had bragged about, or the recipe for the Brazilian blowout. If she could get someone to translate it, maybe she could make it herself and save a few hundred dollars a month.

She looked outside. The wind had picked up. A plastic Wal-Mart bag, dirt, and leaves blew past the door. Besides the wind, the only thing she heard was the distant laughter from the playground. There was nothing to indicate anyone was near the apartment. With shaking, clumsy fingers, she put the book in her purse and zipped it closed.

Eight minutes.

She sat back at the table and willed her hands to stop shaking. Stealing from a woman named Crazy Jade was stupid. But if she didn't want someone to take it, Jade shouldn't have left it on her bookshelf with a stranger in her house. The time ticked away while she tapped her nails on the table and thought about all the reasons why Jade didn't need the book anymore.

Ten minutes. Ashley almost thought to wash it out, but Chantel had always left it in for twenty minutes. Naw, her hair was too nappy for only ten minutes, she decided. She needed at least fifteen minutes to get her roots straight. Where the hell was Crazy Jade, though? For $350 she shouldn't have to wash her own hair.

After fifteen minutes; Ashley gave up on Jade and stepped into the kitchen. She had been in dozens of apartments growing up, but Vista Apartments had the smallest kitchen she'd ever seen. The sink stood directly across from the electric stove, and she could barely stand without bumping into the oven.

She washed her hair using the gloves, shampoo and conditioner left on the counter next to the Dawn dishwashing liquid. As the warm water and shampoo cleansed her scalp, she ran her hands through her hair expecting to catch her fingers on a few stubborn tangles that usually remained after a blowout. But her fingers maneuvered seamlessly through her hair. Zero pain. "Wow, this is better than what I had before," Ashley said out loud, wishing there was someone in the room she could share her excitement with.

After three washes, taking care to remove all the chemicals, she put a towel on her head and stood. Her breath caught in her throat. Wet black strands of hair filled the sink. She was hardly able to see the dull metal basin underneath.

"Damn, I guess I shouldn't have left it in for so long."

Ashley washed the stray hair down the drain before she ran to the bathroom mirror. She breathed a sigh of relief. Thankfully, there was still plenty of hair on her head. A few strands of fell out while she ran her hands through her hair, but that was normal. It happened every time she had a Brazilian blowout. This was just a bit more than usual.

"What's going on?" Jade stood in the hallway.

Ashley frowned, trying to cover up the fact she had been scared. "It took you long enough."

"I've been gone for almost thirty minutes, are you just now washing that stuff out?"

"No, I've been waiting for the past twenty minutes."

"Then why is your hair still soaking wet?"

Ashley rolled her eyes and shrugged. "I don't know."

Jade looked like she was going to argue, so Ashley cut her off. "Are you going to blow dry my hair or not?"

Ashley tried to walk out of the bathroom, but Jade grabbed her arm.

"How long did you leave it in?" Jade asked sternly.

"Fifteen minutes," Ashley said, shaking away Jade's hand.

"I told you ten."

"You should have come back earlier. What were you doing anyway?"

"Saving an old lady's life," Jade said.

"I paid you to do my hair. I shouldn't have to wash it myself."

Jade lifted an eyebrow. "Because your hair is more important than someone's life?"

"No, it's not, but I paid you," Ashley said embarrassment replacing anger. "Besides, what harm can an extra five minutes do anyway?"

"Nothing. I hope," she said sarcastically. "Come on, you paid me to do your hair. Let's get it done."

Forty minutes later, when her hair was properly blow-dried and flat-ironed, Ashley paid Jade and left the stuffy apartment. The wind had died down, and only a slight breeze remained. It jostled her hair, and the light prickling on her neck made her smile. Her hair had never been so weightless that it moved and then effortlessly settled back in place.

"Hey, Ashley. Where are you coming from?"

Ashley turned to see Sean, the young cutie who lived in the apartments. She had dated his best friend's brother before she met Ebony's father. "What's up, Sean?" she asked.

"You do something different to your hair?" he asked.

"Jade straightened it for me," she said, patting her hair.

"You know she's crazy, right? You shouldn't be messing with her."

"You think she's a voodoo priestess, too?" Ashley laughed. "Sean, you're too smart to believe in that kind of stuff."

"Voodoo is a religion rooted in the worship of ancestors, and Jade does not worship her ancestors. She's evil, and you need to stay away from her."

Ashley rolled her eyes. "You is crazy. She's not the devil, and she's not evil." She thought about the book she'd stolen, and its cryptic writing. Maybe he knew something about the book. But she couldn't ask him about it without admitting she stole it. "I'm grown. I don't need you watching out for me."

"Just be careful," he said.

He looked genuinely concerned, and Ashley softened. "Why are you so worried?"

Sean took a deep breath and looked back towards Jade's apartment. "Nothing," he said. "Just be careful. If you don't have to mess with her, don't."

She patted his arm to reassure him. "I'll leave her alone. I promise." She got what she needed anyway. And if she could figure out what language the book was written in, she could make her own blowout.

Ebony slept snuggled in the nook of her grandmother's arms. They both Cora and Ebony slept with downturned lips that made it seem like they were both having bad dreams.

Cora's eyes flashed opened. "Girl, what the hell are you doing?" She said through gritted teeth, keeping her voice so Ebony wouldn't. "You scared the hell out of me."

"Sorry," Ashley said. "You guys looked so peaceful. I didn't want to wake you."

Cora answered with a grunt and carefully sat up. The child whined with sleepy annoyance and clung to Cora tighter.

"Sweetie, you ready to go?" Ashley asked, bending down and lifting Ebony into her arms.

Ebony mumbled a 'no', but she never opened her eyes.

Cora went to the kitchen and poured herself a cup of water, and took a long drink. "Your hair looks good."

"You think?" Ashley shifted Ebony in her arms.

"It looks damn good." Cora put her cup on the kitchen cabinet and ran her hands through Ashley's hair. "It has White Girl Flow. Damn. I can't believe how smooth it feels. I told you Crazy Jade knows her stuff."

"Yeah, she did a good job. She charged a lot, though."

"She ain't cheap." Cora brought her hands to her mouth and gasped. "Baby, your nose is bleeding."

"What?" Ashley put Ebony back on the couch and touched her nose. Her hand came away covered in blood.

Cora passed her a napkin, and with trembling hands, Ashley tried to stop the blood.

"You need to sit down and lean your head back," Cora said with a concerned, commanding voice. Ashley couldn't help but be touched by her mother's rare show of worry.

"No, no," Ashley pulled the napkin from her nose. "It stopped. See." She was relieved to see her wishful thinking had been the truth. The napkin was soaked, but no more blood flowed.

"Since when you do get nose bleeds?" Cora's question was filled with fear and suspicion.

"I think it's just the heat," Ashley said. "Jade's apartment was hot, and she had the door opened the entire time."

Cora sucked her teeth and narrowed her eyes, but before she could ask another question, Ebony woke up.

"Hi, Mommy," she said getting up from the couch and reaching for Ashley. "Oooh," Ebony said after Ashley picked her up. "Look at your hair. It's so beautiful, Momma."

Ashley smiled, trying to forget about Sean's warning and her bloody nose. "Thank you, baby. You ready to go home and see your daddy?"

"Yeah." Ebony yawned, resting her head on her mother's shoulder while affectionately running her fingers through Ashley's straightened hair.

When they finally made it home, Ashley covered her hair with a do-rag and a plastic shopping bag, before she took a short shower. Afterwards, she put Ebony in the bathtub. As her daughter played with the bubbles and her water toys, Ashley stared in the mirror and experimented with different hairstyles. It looked best when it was down and flowing. But she could pull off bangs, ponytails, and buns on the days she wanted a change.

When Ebony started complaining about her skin turning gray and getting wrinkled, Ashley forced herself away from the mirror, lifted Ebony out of the tub, and dressed her in a pair of Teletubbies pajamas.

Steven, Ebony's dad, was due home in an hour, and she wanted everything to be perfect. She sat the child at the kitchen table surrounded by three teddy bears, a white Malibu Barbie, and a coloring book. While she colored, Ebony asked the toys about their day. She mimicked different voices for each toy. Cora said that was a sign Ebony needed a little brother or sister, but Ashley wasn't having any more kids if she had her way. One kid was enough. She hadn't had any brothers or sisters and she turned out just fine.

"Momma, what are we having for dinner?" Ebony scribbled with a blue crayon over Cookie Monster's face.

"We are having fried pork chops, macaroni, and green beans." Ashley reached into the top cabinet and grabbed a box of macaroni and cheese, opened it, placed the sauce package on the countertop, and poured the pasta into a boiling pot of water. "It's your daddy's favorite meal," she said, more to herself than Ebony.

Jodeci's "Forever My Lady" played on the cassette player. She and Steven had slow danced to this song the first time they met while at a house party. She bobbed her head and swayed her shoulders to the beat while she stirred away the clumps out of the macaroni. The air smelled of fried pork chops and black cherry incense from the air freshener plugged into the wall.

Ashley poked a fork in the last two chops frying in the grease. They were white all the way through, so she took them out of the pan and placed them on a napkin to catch the oil. As she stirred the macaroni to the beat of the song, something red dropped into the water. Before she could bring her hands to her nose, a steady stream of blood fell into the pot, turning the water and the macaroni pink.

She took her hand away from her nose, hoping the blood had stopped, but it still gushed like a waterfall. The flow created a pool of blood in the palm of her hand. She reached for a dish towel, but a sharp pain shot through her head. The feeling was so intense it took her breath away and made her knees buckle. She grabbed the counter to stop her fall while fireworks danced behind her eyelids. When she opened her eyes, she saw streaks of blood on the counter, but vibrant lights were still playing havoc with her sight.

She tried to call out to Ebony, but no sound escaped her lips. Jodeci singing about getting to know her suddenly felt like the theme song for her death. "Ebony," she managed to say, just as another explosion of pain sent her to the floor, turning everything into nothing.

ANDRE

Hair is the first thing. And teeth the second. Hair and teeth. A man got those two things he's got it all." — *James Brown*

Andre picked his high-top fade three times before he patted it down, making sure the top was good and flat.

He put the black hair pick on the back of the bathroom counter and studied his reflection. Smudges of toothpaste and specks of brown hair gel were splattered on the mirror. He hurriedly wiped the stains with a wet piece of tissue, threw the paper into the toilet and looked in the mirror again.

Andre bit his lip and nodded. His hair looked damn good.

He stared at his black basketball shorts and his freshly starched white t-shirt. Last night, he'd spent thirty minutes ironing and starching the shirt while he watched music videos on BET in the living room.

His clothes looked damn good.

He peered in the mirror again to makes sure there were no crust in the creases of his eyelids and no boogers in his nose.

He blew his breath into his hand. It smelled good and minty.

"Get out of the bathroom, Andre!" His brother screamed.

"I just got in here." Andre shouted in return.

"You been in there for thirty minutes. Hurry the hell up."

"I just got in here!" he said absently, while he stared in the mirror and patted the top of his box.

"Hurry up!"

"Damn." Andre stepped over his dirty pajamas and opened the bathroom door.

Malik, Andre's older brother, stood on the other side. "You gonna make me late for work."

"You got a job. You need to move out," Andre said.

Sam took his hands and pressed down on Andre's hair. "I ain't going nowhere. I'm going to stay here to mess with you for the rest of your life."

"I hate you," Andre said, ducking and trying to get away to protect his hair.

"Whatever." Sam laughed and slammed the bathroom door.

Andre bucked up to the closed door for one last show of dominance before he walked into the living room.

Koko and Kali, his two little sisters, were sitting in front of the television watching cartoons and eating cereal. They giggled as two lab rats planned to take over the world. While they laughed, large drops of milk and cereal fell out of their mouths and onto the carpet.

"Where is Momma? She's gonna get y'all for eating in the front room." Andre imagined the bugs that would pounce on the area once the girls were gone and the lights were out.

"She went to see Uncle Teddy. And you need to mind your own business," said Koko or Kali, Andre couldn't tell them apart most days.

They were born eleven months apart. One was seven, and the other eight, but they had the same brown skin tone, and they were almost the same height. To make it worse, their mother dressed them alike and did their hair exactly the same. Since he couldn't tell them apart, he just called them the worsesome twins.

"I would come over there and whoop yo' ass, but I ain't got time for y'all." Neither he nor Sam had been allowed to eat in the front room when they were their age.

Deciding to ignore them, he went to the kitchen to make a bowl of cereal. He took the box of Rice Krispies from the counter, opened the fridge, and his heart sank. "Y'all drunk all the milk!" he yelled.

The girls replied with more giggling and probably more food falling onto the floor.

"Ugh. I don't even know why Momma had to go and have any more kids. Damn brats."

"I'm telling Momma you cussed," both Koko and Kali shouted.

Stomach growling, he searched the fridge for more food, but he knew it was useless. It was the end of the month and it would be two more days until they got more food stamps. Until then, he was straight out of luck. He slammed the refrigerator closed. The force sent glass jars of miracle whip, grape jelly, and salad dressing rattling against each other.

"Ooh... I'm telling Momma you broke the icebox!" one of them shouted.

"Shut up!" Andre walked to the living room. It smelled of clothes detergent and dryer sheets. His mother had washed last week's laundry two days ago. The clothes were never folded, so they were piled on the couch. He'd hidden his basketball in the mess of clothes, towels, and underwear so his sisters wouldn't find it. He dug through the clothes, grabbed his ball, and left the apartment.

It was only eleven o'clock and the heat hadn't picked up yet. He needed to get to the court before all the other wanna-be ballers came out, but damn. He knew from experience he couldn't kick ass without eating. Andre sighed and surveyed Vista Apartments. He had homies all through here, but most of them had empty fridges at the end of the month too. Sean was the only person he knew with parents that were not on food stamps or weren't just flat broke. But every time Andre stepped into their house, Mr. Accra, Sean's dad, looked at Andre like he had crap on his face.

He sprinted towards the parking lot, and a smile crept across his face. Mr. Accra's tan Toyota Camry was nowhere in sight. That meant his evil ass was gone. Good.

He walked the few feet to Sean's apartment and knocked.

"Why you knocking on my door like the police?" Sean wiped the sleep from his eyes. He wore baggy, red boxers and no shirt. He was a few shades lighter than Andre with small eyes like the super model Tyson Bedford, and all the damn girls loved him for it.

Andre shoved past Sean. "Wake up. It's almost eleven."

Sean's apartment was not meant for the living. All of their furniture was white and wrapped in plastic. There were no specks of dust on the furniture or bookshelves. There were no clothes out of place. Mr. Accra was a male nurse, and their apartment always felt like a sterile hospital.

"It's Saturday," Sean said as if that was an excuse to still be in bed.

"What you got to eat?" Andre placed his basketball near the front door before he went to the kitchen and opened the refrigerator.

"I don't know. Take what you want. I'm going to get dressed."

While Sean disappeared into the back of the apartment, Andre dug through the fridge. Jackpot! He pulled out eggs, bread, and the butter and put them on the counter next to the stove. "You want a fried egg sandwich?" he shouted.

"Hell naw!" Sean screamed from the back.

"Whatever." Andre rummaged through the cabinets until he found a frying pan.

Just as Andre sat at the kitchen table with his finished sandwich and a glass of water, Sean returned smelling of toothpaste and Irish Spring soap. He sat across from Andre at the dining room table. He had changed out of his boxer shorts and into a pair of black jeans with no crease down the middle and a wrinkled black t-shirt. How he got so much attention from the girls, Andre had no idea.

53

"Your dad at work?" Andre asked.

"Yeah. You already know."

"I heard your two girlfriends got into it yesterday." Andre bit into his sandwich. The yolk, salty and delicious, burst into his mouth.

Sean rolled his eyes and leaned back. "Don't remind me. That was crazy."

Andre laughed and a piece of egg shot across the table. "Man, you got the finest light-skinned girl in the school and you messing it up for Shemeya."

"It ain't like that. Besides. Shemeya is fine. You just think every girl got to be white or light-skinned."

"Anyway, can I ask Latreece out now?" Andre asked in between a bite of his sandwich.

"Hell no," he sneered. "We haven't broke up. She'll calm down in a few days."

"That's not what I heard," Andre said, thinking of lines that might work on Latreece.

Andre finished the last of the sandwich and drank his glass of water in one gulp.

"You coming to the basketball court?"

"No, I got stuff to take care of," Sean said.

"Since when do you do anything on Saturdays except play ball?"

He lifted his shoulders and ignored the question.

"Your loss." Andre picked up his ball from the floor, opened the front door but stopped abruptly. A woman with long hair and a voluptuous ass headed towards the parking lot. Her hair flowed past her shoulders in a black cascade. She wore a leather jacket and tight stonewashed jeans. "Damn,

Sean, is that Ashley? My brother's ex is looking good." It must be her. Ashley was the only light-skinned chick with class around here. But she usually wore a ponytail to hide her nappy hair.

Sean ran to the door in less than a second, looking at Ashley's ass right next Andre. But then she turned, and they both jumped back.

"Damn." Andre's stomach twisted with fear and shock. He'd been correct. It was Ashley. She looked good from the back, but when she turned, her face was a different story. Her eyes were sunken into her face, and they were surrounded by black-blue circles that contrasted sharply with her pale skin.

"Has she been doing crack?" Andre asked, half-joking and half-serious.

Andre looked at Sean. His eyes were unreadable.

Ashley turned back towards the parking lot and walked away. As she disappeared, the twisting in his belly began to unwind. "I'm about to go play ball. You coming?"

Sean sighed and looked from the spot Ashley had been. "No. Like I said. I'm staying in today."

How the hell did someone go from fine-as-hell to crack-head so fast? Andre wondered. She must've been doing that for years without anyone knowing. He shook his head in pity while he dribbled his ball past the swimming pool to the basketball court.

A silver boom box sat on the grass and belted out Tupac's "Brenda's Got A Baby" while Andre surveyed his competition. There were six guys on the court playing 3 on 3 with no one on the sidelines waiting to get tagged in. While he waited, he noticed two girls sitting near the playground. They sat on the picnic tables watching a kid in red overalls climbing on the jungle gym. They must have been new because he'd never seen them before. One of the girls had pale blotchy skin and strawberry-blonde hair. The other was a blond with smooth tanned skin.

"You playing or what?" Raymond asked, sweat clung to his dark skin and glistened off the bald spot on the top of his head.

"Take your old ass home." Andre placed his ball on the grass and stepped onto the court.

"You can talk noise now, but I'll kick your ass when I get back," Raymond said with a labored breath.

"Whatever," Andre said.

During the game, the girls smiled, giggled, and turned away every time he looked over. He wondered if they were from the neighborhood or new to the apartments. The longer he played, the more curious he became. He was relieved when he saw Benita, Latreece's cousin, talking to them. She gave him an excuse to walk over.

"You're up," Andre said to Raymond, who had been drinking grape Kool-Aid and talking noise from the sidelines.

"You scared? Why you leaving?" Raymond asked, setting his drink on the grass.

"Man, I'll be back." Andre dismissed the insult with the wave of his hand.

As he approached, the two girls laughed and looked away; trying to pretend they didn't see him coming, but Benita eyed him coldly, scowling as he approached.

"What's up, Benita?" he asked.

"What's up, Andre?"

"Who are your friends?"

"None of your damn business," Benita said.

He turned from her, still feeling her gaze on the side of his face. "Where y'all from?" he asked the shorter girl with the tan.

"We just moved in," she replied.

She was even prettier up close, Andre realized. "What's your name?" he asked, deepening his voice.

She glanced away for a moment, but then she looked at him and smiled. "I'm Julia."

He couldn't remember the last time a girl made him feel this good just by smiling. "I'm Dre. Like Doctor Dre." His heart pounded, but he kept his face straight.

"It's Andre," Benita said, "not Dre. Why are you over here anyway? They don't care what your name is." She sneered and looked him up and down as if to say she knew exactly why he was here, and she wasn't going to make it easy for him. Benita was dark but pretty. She usually wore her hair down, but she'd gotten it braided a few weeks ago, and it hung down her back making her look like Janet Jackson in *Poetic Justice.*

"Man, I'm just trying to be friendly." Damn. He should have come over when Benita had left. He had forgotten the girl tried to get with him when Sean and Latreece first hooked up. He had turned her down. She was nice and all, but he hadn't been interested.

"Take your skinny, slanky ass back to the basketball court 'cause nobody wants you over here," Benita said, her braids swinging as she rolled her neck.

From the corner of his vision, he saw Julia and the other girl giggle.

"You're just jealous cause nobody wants your ass," he said, acting fast to save face.

"Forget you. Why is it whenever the white girls come our here your fake ass be all over 'em?" Rage flashed in Benita's eyes.

"Cause y'all black girls is loud and look like cockroaches," Andre said, matching Benita's anger with his own.

Her mouth fell open, and she turned gray. She looked as if she'd just swallowed a fly.

Andre looked around. It seemed like the entire apartment complex had gone quiet as he realized what he'd just said.

He hadn't noticed before, but Crazy Jade and her son were a few feet away. Her son sat on the swing uselessly kicking his legs. Jade mother held the metal chain preventing him from moving while she stared at Andre.

"I'm telling your momma," Benita said, jabbing her finger into his chest, her moment of speechlessness gone. The entire complex came alive again with the squeaking sneakers on the basketball court and grunts from the ballers. Crazy Jade to push her son again, but she still stared at Andre.

"I was just kidding," he said to Benita, but she had already stalked away, anger rolling off her in waves.

The other girls had left, too. They knew better than to get in between an argument with two black folks. He should have ran after Benita to try to get her to stay quiet, but he knew a lost battle when he saw one. But he could salvage his conversation with Julia. He started after her, but something, someone, grabbed his arm.

He looked down to see Crazy Jade. *She'd just been at the swings. How did she get here so quickly?*

He tried to pull his arm away, but her grip was as strong as a vice. "Excuse me," he said, pulling his arm away and attempting to be polite. He was in enough trouble already. The last thing he needed was for his mother to find out he was rude to an adult, also.

She held on, refusing to loosen her grip. "All black woman look like cockroaches?" she asked.

"No, I was . . ."

"Isn't your mother black?"

"I'm sorry, Miss Jade," Andre laughed nervously. "I was just talking noise. I didn't mean it."

"If all black girls look like cockroaches, and your mother is black, then that makes you a cockroach." Her face was twisted like she was trying to do a difficult math problem in her head.

"I was just kidding," he said. "Benita was talking smack to me first."

She narrowed her eyes and said something in a language he couldn't understand.

But he knew enough to be scared. He tried again to pull his arm away, but her grip was too strong. Panic bubbled in his belly. Just as he was about to scream, she let go. He fell to the ground, landing hard on his butt.

Jade's copper eyes glared down at him before she turned to her son, who still sat on the swing pumping his legs up and down.

"Come on, baby," she said. "Let's get inside. There are one too many cockroaches out here."

Andre's heart pounded as he sat on his ass and watched Crazy Jade and her son walk away. *What the hell just happened?*

He closed his eyes and willed himself to relax. Had she cursed him? Everyone said she was a witch, but witches don't exist. She was only trying to scare him. Why would an evil witch walk around the hood with a kid? If she was a witch, why was she broke just like everyone else? A real witch would have enough power to have money. If she lived here, there must not be anything magical or special about her.

Raymond walked over with a grin on his face and a cup in his hand. The smell of the liquor reached Andre before Raymond did.

"What did Crazy Jade do to you?" Raymond asked laughing.

"Man, she crazy." Andre stood and patted the dirt and grass from the back of his shorts. "You see where those girls went?"

Raymond shook his head and grimaced. "Them white girls?

"Yeah."

"Them girls are gonna get your ass in some serious trouble one day."

"It ain't the 1950s. Lots of black dudes in school got white girls and ain't nobody been lynched." Andre remembered the hurt on Benita's face and the crazy way Jade spoke to him. He shook his head, deciding to concentrate on more important issues. "Whatever. Did you see where they went?"

"I saw them hanging around there yesterday." Raymond pointed to the far end of the complex, past the playground.

Without another word, Andre ran in the direction Raymond had pointed. He rounded the corner and slowed when he found who he was looking for. Julia sat alone on the stairs, almost like she was waiting for him.

He walked towards her and wiped the sweat from his forehead. "What's up?" he asked. "I thought I'd lost you."

She smiled with perfectly straight, white teeth. "I thought you would be getting your butt whooped by your momma."

He laughed. "No. My mom is cool. She knows I like to talk noise." Andre lied. His momma was gonna kick his ass when she found out what he'd said. But Julia didn't need to know that.

"Do you really think black girls look like cockroaches?" she asked incredulously. "That's harsh."

"No. I was just trying to rag on Benita. I didn't think before I spoke." He grinned. "I talk too much sometimes."

She nodded, looking as if she was giving his answer serious thought. He couldn't tell if she was happy to hear he didn't think black girls looked like cockroaches or disappointed.

"There isn't anything wrong with them," he explained. "Benita liked me, but I wasn't interested. That's why she was talking all that noise."

Julia nodded. This time, she looked more bored than anything.

He sat beside her on the stairs. The sun had heated the step, and it was almost too hot to sit on. "Why haven't I seen you before?"

"I just moved in last week."

After thirty minutes, Andre learned Julia was a sophomore, one year below him, her first day at school would be Monday, and he'd left with her phone number.

It was near ten and dark outside before Andre started the trek to his apartment. He'd thought about spending the night with Sean instead of going home. But he had a feeling his mother would track him down and beat him in front of the entire apartment complex.

He stood outside the door, took a deep breath and turned the knob. He peered inside, hoping his mom would be already in bed. The lights and the TV were off. He couldn't remember the last time he'd stepped into the house before midnight without a television show or videos blaring in the background. The laundry from earlier was gone. He winced when he saw his mother sitting on the couch in the darkness.

"Sit down, boy," she ordered.

Wordlessly, he closed the door, switched on the lamp in the living room, and sat next to her.

"I'm s. . ." he began, ready to defend himself.

"Shut up," Pam Jackson ordered. "Is what Benita said true?" She must have just taken a shower because she wore a red bathrobe, and she smelled of cocoa butter lotion. A thick, see-through plastic shower cap covered the large pink foam rollers she had in her hair.

"Momma, she was talking smack all up in my face." His voice sounded too loud and defensive even to him.

"Did you tell Benita that black girls look like cockroaches?" Her voice was steady and sounded as if she hoped he would deny it.

He clenched his jaw and focused his gaze on where he imagined the worsesome twins had wasted their sugary cereal, debating rather he should tell the truth or not.

"Did you!" she shouted, startling him out of his thoughts.

"Yes," he muttered, condemning himself. "But I didn't mean it."

"You fixed your mouth to say it. You must think there is some truth to it." She turned to him. Her eyes were hard and glistening with tears. "Every time I go to the grocery store, people look at me like I'm a parasite because I use food stamps to feed my family. When I go out in public with four kids and no man in sight, I'm treated like a welfare queen. Outside of this house, I'm nothing but a cockroach to people who don't know me. To come home and learn that my son has said those words to another black woman." She wiped the tears from her face. "This is a hundred times worse than being treated like crap by everyone outside of my house. They don't matter to me, but you did." She stood and began walking to the back of the house.

"But, Momma."

She stopped. "I know I'm not perfect. I know we don't have nothin'. But I didn't raise you to disrespect women, especially black women."

"But, Momma!" his voice cracked while tears fell onto his face.

"Shut up!" she shouted. "I don't want to hear or see you anymore tonight. You're lucky I don't throw you out onto the streets."

He closed his mouth and watched his mother walk into her room.

Left alone, he longed for an ass whooping with a switch while she cursed him out. Because he knew the next day, she'd be herself again. She'd still be his mother. But as he watched her leave, the reassurance she would still love him was no longer there.

His mother didn't say a word to him for the rest of the weekend. Whenever she looked his way, she scowled and rolled her eyes. To pile guilt on top of trouble, the worsesome twins, after hearing what he'd said to Benita, had asked if he thought they looked like cockroaches. His automatic response was to say yes and brush them off, but he hesitated.

"Don't y'all already know you're pretty?" They were always showing off their new hairstyles and prancing around

64

in identical outfits, looking for compliments from anybody who believed they were twins. How could they not know?

"Yeah, but do you think we look like cockroaches?" one of them asked. "We're black girls. And you said black girls look like cockroaches." They stared at him with a steady, hard gaze like they already knew they wouldn't like his answer.

He bent to one knee. For the first time since they were babies, he studied them, taking in their dark brown skin. Koko had a tooth missing in the front, and Kali had no front teeth on the top or bottom. Both had their mother's wide nose and large eyes. But even with missing teeth, they were beautiful.

"Koko and Kali," he said. "You're the most beautiful girls I've ever seen. Y'all hair is always on point. And your clothes be styling more than anyone else in these apartments, even mine. Nah, y'all don't look like no damn cockroaches."

They narrowed their eyes and pulled away from him. Then Kali, slightly taller than Koko, rolled her neck, and said, "Yeah, I know I'm fine."

"Me too." Koko imitated Kali's head roll and snapped her fingers three times. They both sauntered away like two supermodels on a catwalk.

Andre leaned against the wall next to the trophy case at the entrance of Gene Autry High School. He had never been so excited for school to start. His mother hadn't said a word to him for the entire weekend, and Malik teased him every time they saw each other. The weekend hadn't been a total let down, though.

Saturday night, he hid in his room and talked to Julia until 1 A.M. Since his mother hadn't officially grounded him, the next day, he met up with Julia, and they walked around the surrounding neighborhood. It took a while and a lot of sweet-talking, but she let him kiss her on the jungle gym at an elementary school. She'd been chewing Big Chew bubble gum, and if he concentrated, he could still taste the cherry-flavored gum on his lips.

"Hey, Andre," Sean said.

"What's up?" Andre said, hoping he'd say what he wanted to say and go away. He was waiting for Julia. He was supposed to be on the bus, but he'd missed it trying to starch and crease his jeans. His brother had to take him to school instead. Because the buses were slow as hell, he'd still made it to school first. Andre wasn't jealous of Sean or anything, but girls always stared at him like he was L.L. Cool J.

"I heard you got into it with Crazy Jade," Sean said.

Andre straightened, steeling himself against the upcoming jokes. "You come to clown me too?"

"Nah. I just want to know what she said to you."

Andre studied Sean, trying to tell if he was lying. "Why?"

"She's been doing some seriously crazy crap, and I'm curious."

Suddenly Andre was curious, too. Why did he care about Crazy Jade? "She said something about if black girls are cockroaches, then I'm a cockroach too." Andre leaned back against the wall.

"Is that it?" Sean asked.

"She mumbled something I couldn't understand. I think she was pretending like she was cursing me. I didn't fall for it. You don't believe in that crap, do you?"

"I don't know, man. How do you feel?"

Andre shrugged. "I feel fine."

"Then, you're probably okay. Just stay away from her, and if anything changes, or you start feeling weird, let me know."

"Yeah. Yeah. Yeah." Andre stepped away from Sean. He had spotted Julia in the crowd of bus kids. Julia made him forget about Crazy Jade, his mother, and cockroaches. She made all of his problems go away.

Clothes. Check. Andre had to tighten the belt on a pair of his brother's old Calvin Klein jeans an extra loop, but they still looked good. He made a mental note to eat more. His mom had gone shopping yesterday, and he planned to spend the next few days eating everything he could get away with.

Hair. Check.

He breathed into his hand to check his breath and cringed. It smelled like rotting meat. Andre quickly put twice as much toothpaste onto his toothbrush and brushed again.

"Andre, hurry up. You've been in there too long," one of the woresome twins shouted through the other side of the door.

"Shut up and wait," he shouted back.

"Get out of the bathroom, Andre," his mother yelled.

Oh crap. "Yes, ma'am." He picked up his dirty clothes and used towels before he quickly left the bathroom. For the past few days, he'd been extra respectful, and he tried his best to do what she wanted before she even had to ask.

With a few minutes to spare before the bus, he threw his backpack on the kitchen counter and opened the refrigerator. His stomach rumbled. There was a fridge full of food, but nothing looked good. Everything seemed cold, sterile, and unappealing.

But something smelled good. He closed the fridge and followed the smell to the trash can. They had fried chicken, yams, and mashed potatoes last night for dinner. The smell of the decaying food made his mouth water.

"What are you doing?"

He jumped away from the trash and looked towards his mother. "Nothing, I was just throwing something away."

"Really? Because that's not what it looked like."

"What else would I be doing with the trash?" he asked, wondering the same thing. *What the hell had I been doing?*

Andre's heart deflated when Julia wasn't at the bus stop. Without her, he had no choice but to think about how he'd almost eaten food out of the trash. He'd been hungry plenty of times, but he'd never been so hungry he wanted to eat garbage.

After the long bus ride, Julia's slender legs were the first things he saw when he entered the school. She had missed the bus this time, and she stood in the same spot he had been yesterday. Her smile made all of his crazy thoughts about eating out of the trash disappear. He returned her smile tenfold. Ordinarily, he would have tried to remain hard and hide his joy, but he needed a distraction. He needed to relax.

He bent to kiss her, but she cringed and moved backward.

"What's wrong?" he asked.

"You're breath smells." Her pink lips twisted into a grimace, and she stepped further away.

He breathed into his hand.

"I don't smell anything," he said. It had smelled bad this morning, but he brushed his teeth twice, and now it smelled fine.

She looked around like she was planning an escape route.

Panic rose in his throat. "What does it smell like?"

Julia covered her nose and mouth. "I have to go," she said in a muffled voice before she half jogged and half ran down the hall, dodging the crowd of students hurrying to their first hour class.

He sniffed his breath again before he smelled his armpits. Nothing.

For the rest of the day, every time Julia saw him, she ducked, dodged, or acted like he didn't exist. He couldn't smell anything wrong, but as an extra precaution, he went to the bathroom and washed his armpits with a damp towel. And in between every class, he'd stick a fresh piece of spearmint gum into his mouth.

The school day went by in a blur while he thought about what could be bothering Julia. Yesterday, the rumor he and Julia were a couple had spread rapidly around the school. Today, when everyone asked about her, he laughed it off and said he didn't do girlfriends. He joked and laughed, pretending to be the clown everyone expected him to be. But he felt like a zombie, a living dead person, going through the motions, pretending his heart wasn't being torn out of his chest.

Andre lived for basketball, but when the day was over, he skipped practice, went home, laid on his bed, and fell mercifully into a dreamless sleep.

Something damp clung to Andre's back, and his stomach rumbled. He didn't know how long he'd been aware of the two warring sensations, but they were finally too uncomfortable to ignore. The bedspread covering his window had fallen and the light from the lamppost beamed onto his face, blinding him. He covered his eyes and sat up. Wondering if he was sick, he touched his forehead, and his hand came away hot and sweaty. .

Except for his rumbling stomach, the apartment was deathly quiet. He looked over to Malik's bed to make sure he wasn't alone in the house. "Malik, did Momma cook?" Andre asked. "Why didn't anyone wake me?"

Malik mumbled something indecipherable, turned over on his twin-sized mattress, and pulled the covers over his head.

Hungry and sweaty, Andre made his way to the kitchen. The smell of something delicious called to him. He followed the scent to the trash can.

As usual, the worsesome twin's eyes must have been bigger than their stomachs because the garbage was filled with leftovers. Limp spaghetti noodles, half eaten pieces of garlic bread covered with lumpy spaghetti sauce, and golden chunks of peaches lay in the trash can. His stomach ached with hunger and desire. He directed his gaze towards the hallway and the living room to make sure no one was coming. Assured he was alone, he reached in and stuffed the harmonious mixture of stale bread, rotting peaches, limp spaghetti noodles and tomato sauce into his mouth. A surge of pleasure started at his tongue and traveled down to his toes while he chewed.

He'd never tasted anything so delicious. He devoured three more pleasurable handfuls before his thoughts fell back on Julia. The pleasure of the food and the joy of being with her mingled in his mind, and he forgot about what happened earlier in school. Andre walked away from the trash, wiped his hands on his pants, picked up the phone mounted on the kitchen wall, and dialed her number.

"Hello," she said, answering on the tenth ring. She sounded sleepy, but she should have been awake waiting for him to call.

"Hey, baby," he said.

"Who is this?"

He deepened his voice. "Andre."

"Oh." She sounded suddenly alert and happy to hear him. Good.

"Dre, I'm sorry. But I think we're going too fast."

"What!" he shouted before he lowered his voice. "What are you talking about?"

"I'm sorry. It's me, not you."

"Hell no, it ain't me. We were fine yesterday."

"I'm sorry. I didn't mean to lead you on."

"Are you seeing someone else?" Andre asked, trying desperately to come up with a reason why she would change her mind so quickly.

"No," Julia said. "I'm just not interested anymore. I need to concentrate on school."

"You're lying. You found somebody else didn't you?" He sounded like a punk, but he couldn't help it.

"No, Dre. It's not like that. I have to go."

"Don't. . ." he began, but she had already hung up.

He didn't remember falling asleep, but he knew his eyes were closed and his face itched. He brought his hand up to scratch, but the itch grew legs, and it scurried across his face.

Begrudgingly, Andre sat up. When he opened his eyes, hundreds of bugs scattered away. He recoiled, screaming when he realized they were all over him. He jumped, hysterically wiping them from his arms, chest, and legs. He felt the crunch and the wetness of dead bugs underneath his bare feet while he tried to get them off. When he pulled them away from his face, they squirmed beneath his fingers.

"Andre, what's wrong? Why are you in here screaming?" His mother stood in the living room. Malik was next to her, holding a baseball bat over his head. His eyes were alert, searching for someone to attack. The worsesome twins peeked from the hallway, too scared to enter the living room.

"There were bugs on me," he said once his breathing slowed enough to speak.

"Why the hell are you sleeping on the front room floor?" Malik asked, lowering his bat.

"I woke up and couldn't go back to sleep." Andre wiped his forehead. Half a dozen bugs were lying motionless on the floor. The rest had disappeared.

"That's what you get for going to bed so early," his mother said. "I tried to wake you, but you wouldn't have it."

With the excitement wearing off, the room began to spin, and Andre collapsed onto the couch. "I don't feel very well," he said.

His mother walked over and put her hand on his head. "You're burning up, baby." She looked worried, almost like she loved him again.

"Go to bed, Dre. You're staying home today. If you're not feeling better by the time I get off work, I'm taking you to the hospital."

LATREECE

Have you ever been in love? Horrible isn't it? It makes you so vulnerable.
It opens your chest and it opens up your heart and it means that someone can
get inside you and mess you up. – Neil Gaiman, *The Sandman*

White floors, white wall, white principal, with mostly white students pretty much summed up Gene Autry High School. Latreece hated this school. She wished she had stayed on the east side and gone to Douglass, one of the only mostly black high schools in Oklahoma City. The school was so popular most of the graduates bought the school's car tags and displayed them on their vehicles like they were a badge of honor. But no, Granny wanted to get out of the hood and away from crackheads, drug dealers, and gangs. So, four years ago, they moved to the northwest side of town. Now, Latreece attended a school in the middle of nowhere, surrounded on three sides by cow pastures.

Latreece slouched in her chair with her arms folded across her chest while Principal Kerr talked to Granny.

"I apologize, Ms. Langston, but we have no choice but to suspend Latreece for a week." Principal Kerr was short and thin. She had a sharp nose, sunken cheeks.

"But," Granny leaned forward, "what about graduation?"

"Assuming she's currently passing, she'll be okay as long as she turns in all her assignments when she returns." The principal looked at Latreece like she was scum and the chances of her graduating were slim. Latreece stared back at the wrinkled woman and sneered. Principal Kerr had her confused with a dummy. Latreece always made sure to do just enough work to keep a C average.

Granny leaned back, her stress level visually dropping from a ten to a five. It was her dream to see Latreece graduate from high school. She didn't want to disappoint her grandmother. She'd stay in school, but as soon as she graduated, she planned on moving to Las Vegas, Los Angeles, or New York. She hadn't decided which state yet, but as long as it wasn't in Oklahoma, she didn't much care. Shoot, most people didn't even know blacks lived here.

Her grandmother nodded towards the principal saying yes ma'am this and yes ma'am that. After every few nods, she would give Latreece the side-eye. *A look that said, damn you girl for making me come up here and have to play nice with this lady.*

"My granddaughter knows better, and this will never happen again," Granny said with a fake smile.

"If she gets into another fight, I'll have no choice but to expel her."

"Why isn't Shemeya here? She started this." Latreece said, tired of staying quiet.

"We haven't been able to track her down. And, according to the other students, you started the fight."

"Okay, can we go now?" Granny said, trying to get Latreece away from the principal before she could get into any more trouble.

Principal Kerr frowned like she swallowed something sour, but she took the hint. "Let me walk you out, Mrs. Langston."

The principal walked them past the secretaries and to the main entrance. "Latreece, we'll see you in a week. Mrs. Langston, you can pick up her homework Monday morning."

"Thank you. I swear this won't happen again."

Latreece rolled her eyes. The sound of her grandmother cowering made Latreece's stomach churn.

As soon as the principal was gone, all docility and smiles left Granny's face and her right eye twitched. "Girl, what is wrong with you!" She slapped Latreece on the back of the head.

"Ouch, Granny," Latreece said, gritting her teeth.

"You know better than to start a fight at school. You know they're craving to kick as many black kids out of this damn place as they can."

"But, Granny . . .

"Don't 'but Granny' me."

Latreece was about to 'but Granny again,' but then she saw them: Sean and Shemeya walking down the hall.

TOGETHER!

Shemeya held a bag of ice to her eye, and she and Sean were so engrossed with each other, they didn't see her.

What. The. Hell?

Latreece stormed towards them, fury boiling in her blood. Sean looked up, eyes wide with recognition and shock.

"This is what you want, Sean?" She was so close, she could see his pores, and she imagined she smelled Shemeya all over him. "I can't even believe I wasted my time on you." She jabbed her finger into his chest. "You is a liar." She pointed at Shemeya. "And you is a ho. Y'all deserve each other."

Having said her piece, Latreece stomped away. Her heart pounded in her ears and tears streamed down her cheeks. Sean was her first love, but she'd be damned if he was going to hurt her again.

Granny gaped, speechless and confused.

"You ready, Granny?" Latreece didn't stop. She left the building, hoping her grandmother would follow.

Latreece waited next to Granny's old-ass green Mercury Valiant and wiped the tears from her cheeks. She felt as if she'd just been stabbed.

When she saw Granny leave the building, she straightened and willed her tears away. She was not this person. She was not the type of girl to cry and lose her crap over some cheating dude.

"Baby, what's wrong? What was that about?" The anger Granny had shown earlier was gone, and now concern and worry etched her smooth brown skin. She was forty-eight and didn't have a single wrinkle. People often thought she was her mother instead of her grandmother.

"Can we just go, Granny?" Latreece looked towards the school. A part of her hoped she would see Sean chasing after her, but the other half hoped he wouldn't. The last thing she wanted was for him to see her crying.

Granny hesitated for a long moment. "Okay," she said, reaching into her purse and digging through bundles of past due bills and other miscellaneous pieces of mail, make-up, and lord knows what else, while she searched for her keys.

"Granny, hurry up," Latreece said anxiously, but it was evident Sean was not going to come after her like this was a damned romantic comedy. Forget him.

"Here they are." Granny pulled out her keys. No less than ten keys were on her key ring, and Latreece knew she didn't know what half of the keys were for.

The car started on the third try and En Vogue's cover of "Something He Can Feel" played through the car's weak speakers. The seats of the Mercury were old, plastic and cracked. They were covered in a thick blanket so they didn't cut into anyone's skin. An empty coffee cup and a discarded Sonic's bag that once held an extra-long chili cheese hot dog, laid on the passenger side floor.

"Now, what's going on?" Granny asked.

"Sean and Shemeya are what's going on," Latreece answered.

"You and Sean were perfectly fine yesterday?"

"That was yesterday. Today, I found out he's just another trifling ass negro, and Shemeya is a lying ass ho."

"Watch your mouth," Granny ordered, but her tone softened a moment later. "He doesn't seem that way, and neither does Shemeya."

"They don't, do they?" It's the innocent people you have to look out for. "They used to have a thing back in the day, and she wouldn't let it end."

"You're in school to graduate, not date. I promised your mother before she died I'd make sure you had a good life. But it can't be all on me. You have to do your part. And that means not getting kicked out of school for stupid stuff."

Latreece sighed and looked out the window. The sky had been overcast and threatening rain all day. It finally made good on its threat, and rain began to pelt the car. Granny switched on the windshield wipers. The cacophony of the rain and wiper blades drowned out the radio.

Whenever Latreece got in any type of trouble or brought home a bad report card, Granny always had to mention Latreece's mother. It wasn't like her mother had been a saint. She had died of a drug overdose. Even when her mother was alive, Latreece had spent most of her time with Granny or her aunts. Anywhere was better than staying with her mother and the woman's endless string of boyfriends. Latreece shook away the bad memories and turned to her grandmother. She was the only constant in her life. Granny had always been able to make all of the nightmares and bad thoughts go away.

"Well, he's crazy because you're much prettier than she is," Granny said.

"Do you think he likes her better because I'm so skinny?"

Granny tightened her grip on the steering wheel. "You're not that skinny."

"Don't lie to me." Latreece insisted.

"What if you are? I raised you to know that you're more than a big ass or big titties."

"You don't understand. Boys don't like skinny girls." Girls with big butts and big titties were all they showed on music videos, and that's what all the boys wanted. Even the white girls at school had bigger butts than her.

"If that boy don't want you 'cause your ass is flat, then you need to leave him alone because he ain't the one for you."

Latreece stared out the window. The world looked distorted and smeared through the rain. "You're right. I don't need him." But it still freaking hurt.

Gary England, Oklahoma's favorite weather man, waxed poetically about the latest group of thunderstorms headed their way. The smell of fried chicken, Velveeta mac and cheese, collard greens, and cigarette smoke filled the apartment.

Reassured that any threat of a tornado was at least thirty minutes away, Latreece turned the station. Martin Lawrence, dressed as a big, ugly, buck-tooth woman, wagged his long neon painted nails in front of a woman's face. Latreece laughed when Shenaenae started windmilling her fists hitting nothing but air.

Since her suspension on Friday afternoon, all Latreece had done was eat, sleep, and watch TV. Vegging out in front of the television was the only thing that helped her forget about Sean's cheating ass. And that was how she planned to spend her entire suspension. Anyone else would gain weight after two days of this, but she'd probably end up weighing less by the time she was allowed back into school.

Thunder rattled the windows, and for two long heartbeats, everything in the apartment went black. Just as the light popped back on, two figures burst through the front door.

Granny ran from the kitchen screaming, and Latreece jumped from the couch, heart beating out of her chest.

"Damn what's wrong with y'all?" asked Aunt Khandi and Aunt Tasha, Granny's other two daughters. Aunt Khandi was a big-boned woman, who always wore red lipstick two shades too bright for her dark skin. Her younger sister had the same dark complexion as Khandi, but Aunt Tasha was shorter with fewer curves.

"Y'all don't know how to knock?" Granny held a greasy fork in her hand and specks of flour stained her chin. "Y'all scared the hell out of us."

"I wasn't scared," Latreece lied, sitting back on the couch with her heart still thumping.

"Girl, please. I heard you scream too," said Aunt Khandi.

"Damn, it's raining hard out there." Aunt Tasha took off her floor length denim jacket stained so dark with rain that it could have easily been soaked with blood instead of water.

"Latreece, where is the tornado right now?" Aunt Khandi asked, paying more attention to the TV than her rain-soaked coat.

Latreece flipped the TV station back to Gary England. "No tornadoes yet. Just rain."

A second later, Benita and Aaliyah came through the door carrying grocery bags. "Why y'all close the door on us? Damn," Benita said.

"Sorry. Y'all slow." Aunt Tasha plopped down on the couch next to Latreece.

"Y'all could have helped get some of the bags out of the car," Aaliyah said.

"Why? I had kids so I wouldn't have to carry another bag or wash another dish in my life." Aunt Khandi took off her coat and hung it behind a chair in the dining room.

Latreece stood, took a bag from Benita and placed it on the kitchen table.

Benita and Aaliyah were thirteen months apart. They had two brothers, but when their parents had split three years ago, the boys had chosen to live with their dad.

As soon as the food was put away, the three girls escaped to Latreece's room to let the adults finish cooking.

Latreece's Gold n' Hot flat iron sat on her vanity table alongside a jar of hair gel and a bottle of Tommy Hilfiger perfume. "Just Kicking It," the R&B song by Xscape, played on the radio, drowning out Gary England's weather report from the living room.

Benita and Aaliyah had brought some weed over to help Latreece with her break up. She took a puff of the joint, closed her eyes, and let herself relax. When Latreece was sixteen, Granny had given them permission to smoke weed, as long as they did it at home and stayed away from hard liquor and hard drugs.

Latreece had been crying on and off for the past two days, whenever the TV shows were not good enough to make her forget about Sean, but as she smoked, the stress and hurt eased.

"You know. I don't mind if black dudes date white girls. But what pisses me off . . ." Benita paused and took the joint from Latreece. "I can't stand the ones who only date white girls. I don't understand that crap." Benita puffed, held her breath for a few seconds and exhaled. She sat at the vanity, above everyone. Her long braids were tied back in one ponytail.

"Why are you worried about Andre? He stupid. Let the white girls have him," Latreece said, thinking more about Sean than Andre, as she sat on her bedspread with her back against the wall.

"He's cute, though." Aaliyah accepted the joint from Benita. "And he is one of the only black dudes that's into something other than being a thug." She sat on the carpet leaning her back against the mattress. It had been a gift from Aunt Khandi after her sons had left with their dad, but there was no bedframe so it sat directly on the floor. Both Aaliyah and Benita were Aunt Khandi's children, but where Benita took after her mother, Aaliyah was more like Aunt Tasha, short and curvy.

The sisters fought like cats and dogs. You could never tell what would set either off. Latreece had wanted a sister until Benita's and Aaliyah's fights became unbearable. From what Latreece observed, Benita was fiercely jealous of Aaliyah. If something good happened to Aaliyah, Benita wouldn't say anything at first, she'd let one or two days pass before she'd blow up over something small and silly. During their fights, there would be windmilling punches, piles of hair, scratched faces, and bloody noses.

"Andre's only interested in girls and basketball. That does not make him a deep thinker," Latreece said.

"But he could make it out of the hood, though," Aaliyah said.

"This is not the hood, and you is shallow," Benita said.

"You don't know hood until you've lived on the east side," Latreece corrected her.

"Yeah, yeah, Latreece, we all know you're hard 'cause you lived a minute on the eastside. But still, I want a man with money. I'm tired of being poor." Aaliyah took a long, exaggerated puff. Instead of relaxing, weed always pepped Aaliyah up and made her more talkative. Her gaze narrowed and settled on Latreece. "So what's up with Sean and Shemeya? Are they official now?"

"Forget Sean," Latreece exclaimed. "If that dreadlocked bitch wants him, she can have him."

Aaliyah said, "I still can't believe Shemeya is that devious. She's always been so cool."

"She can have him if he's that easily got," Latreece said. Granny said time heals all wounds. Now, Latreece just had to do her time. She puffed the joint, the heat burned her chest, but she held it there, reveling in the pain before she exhaled.

Through the haze of smoke, Latreece focused on Aaliyah. "Why does your skin look so different?"

Aaliyah's smile lit up her face. "It's about time you bitches noticed. I went to Crazy Jade, and she gave me an herb that cleared my skin."

"Granny is gonna get you once she finds out. You know how she feels about witchcraft. Sean even told me to stay away from her," Latreece said.

"Forget Sean. Witch or not, the stuff she gave me cleared my skin." Aaliyah turned to the vanity and ran her hands along the side of her face, admiring her reflection in the mirror.

"I don't know if it's science or witchcraft, but I heard she turned Old Mr. John's gray hair black, and she gave Miss Dorothy something to help her lose twenty pounds," Benita added.

"But what about your soul?" Latreece asked in a low whisper, thinking Granny would come through the door at any moment and condemn them for talking about witchcraft.

Benita shook her head. "The weed is making you paranoid. Granny is superstitious. You can't believe everything she says."

Latreece perked up. "Do you think Crazy Jade can make my butt bigger?"

Benita and Aaliyah exchanged glances before they burst out laughing. "I don't think there is anything you can do about that crap," Aaliyah said. "Besides, if you want to be a model and make money, the last thing you want is a big butt."

Monday morning, on her first full day of suspension, Latreece found herself outside of the witch's apartment. Granny left to refill her diabetes medicine. The storms from Saturday night were long gone, and the sticky, hot weather had returned. Industrial sized lawnmowers whirred somewhere near the back of Vista Apartments, and the air was thick with the smell of fresh cut, wet grass and exhaust fumes.

Latreece mustered her courage, took a deep breath, and knocked on apartment 180.

The woman on the other side of the door wore a pair of jeans and a white t-shirt. "What do you want?" Jade asked.

"Yeah...Uh...," Latreece's voice quivered. "I wanted to know if you could help me with something."

Jade narrowed her eyes. "You're the girl that was messing with Shemeya the other day."

"Yeah. So?" Latreece folded her arms across her chest.

"What do you want?" Jade straightened and squared her shoulders.

It was too late to leave now. "I heard you could do things?" Latreece said.

Jade laughed, her freckles crinkling along her nose and cheeks. "You can't afford me."

"I have money." Latreece pulled out the two hundred and fifty dollars she'd been saving since her birthday. She had planned to use it for her and Sean's prom night, but that plan was dead and buried.

The humor disappeared from Jade's face, replaced with greed. "What is it you need?"

"Can you make my butt and chest bigger?"

Jade studied the money in Latreece's hand. "If I told you for two-hundred and fifty dollars I could grant any one of your heart's desires, would you still wish for bigger assets?"

"Yes," Latreece answered. She should have said the nice thing and wished for world peace. But there was no such thing. It was a hypothetical question beauty queens were asked in pageants. Latreece wasn't Miss America, and the world would never be happy. People like her mother would always choose pain. "But I'm giving you money, so that means you can't have my soul, or curse my granny, or anyone else in my family." The world may never be at happy, but having a bigger butt would get her closer to having inner peace.

"What exactly do you think I am?" Jade asked, her voice filled with curiosity and humor.

"A witch who helps some people but might curse others?" Latreece had thought of everything Granny had told her and remembered all the movies about witches she'd ever seen. She'd decided on a simple plan to make sure Crazy Jade wouldn't be able to curse her.

"Why come here, if you think I'd put a curse on you?"

"I don't know. Everyone comes here. And you're always nice to your son. You can't be all that bad," Latreece answered honestly.

"Come in and give me the money." Crazy Jade's shirt showed her midriff. Her stomach was flat, but stretch marks crept past the top of her jeans, but at least she had a nice sized butt.

Granny's threats about witchcraft and Sean's warnings about Crazy Jade were playing on repeat in her head, but she ignored them and stepped inside.

Her apartment was humid and muggy, but at least it was clean. She had one couch and no television.

"Turn around and let me see your butt," Jaded ordered.

Self-consciously, Latreece did a slow turn, trying not to cringe as she felt Jade's gaze probe her body.

"Have you tried just eating more?" Jade asked.

"Yes, but nothing happens."

"Hold on." Jade turned towards the bookshelf in the living room. The top shelves were filled with normal non-witchy things like *Where The Sidewalk Ends* and even a few black romance novels. But Jade wasn't looking at the books on top. She was crouched towards the bottom shelf where the books had no titles. Instead, they had brown paper bag book covers. "My book is gone," she said after a few minutes of uncomfortable silence.

"Does that mean you can't help me?" Latreece asked, disappointed.

Jade furrowed her brow before she snapped her finger. "Wait here." She walked into the back of her apartment and returned a moment later with some type of potato.

"What's that?" Latreece asked, apprehensively.

"This is maca root." Jade caressed it as if it were a baby. It was about half the size of Jade's hand, and the color was ugly, something between the brown of a potato and a purple beet. Flecks of dirt covered the root as if it had just been pulled from the ground.

"What the hell is a maca root?" Latreece asked.

"It's something that will give you junk for your trunk," Jade said. "But you'll still have to eat."

"I told you. I have and it didn't do anything."

"Believe me, this root will help, but you'll still have to eat more."

"I'm paying two hundred and fifty dollars for a root. What makes you think I can't go and get this myself?"

"You could try, but my remedies are unique."

Latreece didn't see how a root could do crap to make her gain weight, but Jade had helped everyone else, so it couldn't hurt to give it a try. "What am I supposed to do with it?"

"After you wash it, take one bite a day. No more than one. And eat three good meals a day. Do everything I say and, you'll have an ass in two weeks."

SEAN

No Good Deed Goes Unpunished. — Oscar Wilde

The aroma of cinnamon and bacon nudged Sean from a restless sleep. He wondered if he'd awakened in the right place. His dad had to be at work before the crack of dawn, so unless Sean cooked it, there was never breakfast in this house.

He hurriedly pulled a pair of jeans over his boxers and walked to the kitchen. William Accra stood in front of the stove cooking turkey bacon on an electric stove. Sean inherited his thick build and six-foot height from his mother's side of the family, so he stood half a foot taller than William. But Sean's copper-colored skin and broad nose were a direct gift from his father.

"What's going on?" Sean asked, sitting at the kitchen table. "Why aren't you at work? Did you lose your job?"

William's shoulders shook as he laughed. "No, I haven't lost my job." He placed a bowl of cinnamon-flavored oatmeal and a plate of bacon on the table. "I have an appointment later."

"Are you okay?" Sean asked.

"It's just a check-up," William said, sitting in front of his food. "I'll have to work late tonight though to make up the time."

Sean nodded, his mouth full of oatmeal.

"Have you seen anything strange in the apartments lately?" William asked.

Sean swallowed his food in one large gulp, almost choking. "No. I haven't noticed anything," Sean lied. He'd seen plenty: Ashley suddenly getting sick, Shemeya walking around with snakes instead of dreads. There were plenty of strange things happening, but he couldn't tell his dad. "Why? Have you noticed something?"

Mr. Accra glanced at the picture of Sean's dead mother hanging above the television. "No, but you would know more than me."

Sean's heart rate increased, but he kept a straight face. "No, Dad. I haven't seen anything like before."

"Good. Good." Mr. Accra sighed, looking like a weight had just been lifted from his shoulders. "You've been pouting around the house all weekend. Did you and Latreece finally break up?"

Sean rolled his eyes.

"Don't roll your eyes at me, boy."

"Sorry," he mumbled, staring at his half-eaten bowl of oatmeal. William thought Latreece was loud-mouthed and over emotional, but that was why Sean was drawn to her. He had been taught to never make waves and always stay quiet, but Latreece would have none of that. She said and did exactly what she wanted. Unfortunately, when she was pissed, she also held a grudge with the same intensity.

His father had loved Shemeya, though. He thought she was smart, reserved, and destined to make something of her life. Sean wondered what William would say if he knew about Shemeya's hair and her habit of wanting to make-out at house parties.

"Latreece is always mad over something, she'll get over it. She always does," Sean said, but he wasn't really sure if she would this time. If it had been anyone but Shemeya, Latreece would have cursed him out and moved on, but she hated Shemeya because Latreece knew how much Sean's father liked the other girl.

A spiky, bloated horny toad, the same color as the concrete, stood outside of Latreece's door. Vista Apartments were full of the creatures, but they usually ran away when someone approached. The lizard sat undisturbed, like a miniature guard dog, with its gut rising and falling with each breath.

"Move," Sean shouted and stomped his foot. It must have been sleeping because it jumped and scurried away with its four short bowed legs. It was lunch time, and he'd told Principal Kerr he would take Latreece her homework. With the small guard gone, he knocked on the door. After a few minutes of pounding with no response, he gave up and started back to his apartment.

He was halfway home when he saw Latreece leaving Jade's apartment. She wore a pair of ripped stonewashed jeans and a t-shirt with the picture of the all black boy band,

New Edition. She held something in her hand. She stared at it like it was a Christmas present.

"What is that?" he asked.

"Oh crap! You scared me." She had been so distracted by what she held, she hadn't noticed him walking beside her.

"I just saw you come from Jade's apartment. I told you to stay away from her. She's crazy."

Latreece's thin lips twisted into a sneer. "You don't control me. What are you even doing here? You're supposed to be in school."

"I brought your homework."

She snatched the papers away from his hand. "I got it. Now, go away."

"What are you holding?" Sean couldn't decide if it looked more like a beet or a turnip, but he knew if it came from Crazy Jade, it was dangerous and Latreece didn't need it.

"Don't worry about it. I'm no longer any of your business."

"Latreece, what you saw between me and Shemeya was nothing. I'm not messing around with her."

"I. Do. Not. Care," she said. "You knew how I felt about Shemeya. Out of respect, you should have stayed away from her. You couldn't do that, so now you need to stay away from me."

"You don't understand."

"I don't need to understand. It's been long enough. We're about to graduate. We need to move on anyway. I hope you, your dad, and Shemeya are happy together."

"Latreece, I love you." He'd never had the guts to say how he felt out loud, but they were powerful words, and maybe it would make her listen.

Her expression softened, and for a moment he thought it worked. But then she hardened again. "Now you love me? Too little too late."

He should have known kind words wouldn't work on her. She was still pissed, and a pissed Latreece jumped on kindness like a tiger pouncing on a gazelle. Still, he couldn't let Crazy Jade get to her.

"Fine, I'll leave you alone. But give me what she gave you first."

"Hell no," she snarled.

Sean grabbed her hand. "Give it to me."

She tried to pull away, but he tightened his grip, hoping the pain would make Latreece drop it. He was not the type to make a girl do anything she didn't want to, but he couldn't let what happened to Shemeya and Ashley happen to her.

Latreece's face contorted with pain and determination as she tried to break free. He was much taller than her, and she was as skinny as a rail, but her will gave her the strength of a bull.

"Is there a problem?" a voice asked from behind.

Sean's blood turned to ice, his breath caught in his throat, and he let go of Latreece's hand.

Latreece grinned from ear to ear as she turned from Sean to Jade. "Cra-. . . Jade, Sean has been warning me to stay away from you. He says you're dangerous."

Jade's gaze felt like a physical thing as she looked him up and down. "Why do you think I'm dangerous?" she asked.

His mouth felt suddenly dry and his tongue felt too big for his mouth. "I didn't say you were dangerous."

"He's lying. That's why he looks so scared," Latreece said with a wry smile that stabbed his heart.

Crazy Jade stepped to him, her freckles jumping on her cheeks. "What do you know about me?"

Sean's heart pounded and black spots danced in and out of his vision. *Run, Sean!* he heard his mother say. He obeyed the voice from his past and ran.

Sean paced in his living room. Fear induced adrenaline coursed through his body. He should have hated Latreece for what she'd done. But Latreece didn't know his past. No one knew. He'd listen to Latreece talk for hours about her mother's death. But he'd lied, and told her his mother had been killed by a mugger.

Eva Accra was born with the cursed ability to see past magical illusions. She saw elves, trolls, and other strange fey creatures, who tried to hide within the human world. They used a magic called glamour to appear human. Most fey were harmless, but a few were dangerous. They were the ones who lived off the pain and suffering of humans. They were the ones who made it a point to kill any human they knew could see past their illusions.

Eva Accra knew her three-year-old son had the same curse when he pulled the ears of a dwarf glamoured to appear as a child.

Luckily, the dwarf had not been dangerous, but Sean was no longer allowed outside. Condemned to the house, he spent his nights studying literature, math, and history with his father. He spent his days learning to recognize and avoid fey creatures. Eva taught him to pretend that the wavering shimmer he saw over a fey's true form was real. He practiced not staring, while not completely avoiding the creatures either.

On Sean's ninth birthday, his mother decided to test him. If he passed, he could attend public school and play outside with other kids. If he failed, assuming he wasn't killed, he would have to endure another year isolated indoors, watching other children play outside from his living room window.

They decided the test would be at Times Square, the busiest place in New York. It was where humans, tourists, and monsters gathered to buy and sell everything from food and clothes to whatever fey bought whenever they believed no humans were looking.

The ruckus of tourists talking about their plans and posing for pictures with Batman, Elmo and Mickey Mouse was like the sounds and sights of freedom to Sean. The smell of pizza, cigarettes, and body odor made him dizzy with happiness.

He ignored the troll with green skin and protruding fangs that sold his caricatures for ten dollars apiece and the talking horse that everyone saw as Batman. He smiled and looked past the old, waif-like creature, glamoured to appear as an old lady while she sold magazines and newspapers. He'd spent most of his life learning about the fey, so these creatures were boring to him. He had not been taught about people, and that was all that interested him. He stared at people with olive-toned skin and eyes the color of sand, black African women with their brightly colored clothes and thick accents. There were guys cruising for guys, girls flirting with boys, and New Yorkers hurrying to and from work.

By the end of the day, he had passed his test, and the following week, he was enrolled in the neighborhood school.

A year and a half later, the Accras took a trip to the Boardwalk to spend the day at the beach. While William Accra dozed under an oversized umbrella, Sean and Eva left to buy peach sodas and candy from one of the cheaper corner stores a few blocks away from the overpriced vendors on the boardwalk. While his mother searched for soda, Sean browsed the aisles. Reggae music played over the loudspeakers and the spicy smell of jerk pork from the street vendor found its way into the store.

The candy was on an aisle next to the bottles of scented oils and air fresheners. He was reaching for a package of sour apple flavored Laffy Taffy when he saw it.

The monster stood in front of the Hershey milk chocolate bars. Sean had seen plenty of fey since being off house arrest, and it had been easy to pretend they were normal humans. But this thing was unlike anything he'd seen or had been taught to avoid. He couldn't tear his gaze away. The weak shimmer around the monster made it appear around the same age of his father. It had neat brown-tipped dreads that stopped at its shoulder.

As Sean stood transfixed, a woman wearing a yellow bikini top and cut-off jean shorts smiled and winked at the monster. She couldn't see that he was actually naked and that black ooze dripped from all of its orifices, including the tip of his penis. His long, thin arms reached past its knees.

It smelled of death and magic, and the scent made Sean's eyes water and his throat tighten. After the creature smiled and winked back at the woman, his gaze found Sean. Without warning, everything went black.

Sean felt like he'd been removed from his body, as if he didn't exist anymore.

The calming warmth of Eva's calloused hand pulled him back from nothingness, reminding his soul it existed.

"Baby, are you okay?" she asked.

Sean blinked away the confusion and looked up. Worry etched the creases of her black-brown eyes.

"Is this your son? I thought he was lost," the monster said with a perfect New York accent.

"No, he's not lost." Eva wore a strained smile. "I'm sorry. I hope he didn't bother you."

"He had an accident," the monster said. They followed its gaze to the yellow puddle pooling on the floor around Sean's sandals.

Eva's smile faltered, showing her own fear in front of the monster.

"I'm sorry, Momma. I couldn't find the bathroom," Sean said, finally remembering his training. His heart thrummed in his chest, but he forced himself to relax. He hoped the monster would believe that he'd blacked out because he was trying not to piss himself and not because he's been so scared his bladder had released.

"Boy, I told you to hold it," Eva said, faking embarrassment and anger. "Now, I have to take you home to get you cleaned up." Without saying another word, she dragged Sean out of the store.

Once they passed the end of the street, they ran. Eva was a big woman with long, sturdy legs, but for once Sean had no problem keeping up with her. They rounded the corner of a building, a few yards from the beach, when the creature dropped out of the sky, blocking their path. It landed on all fours with a wicked toothy grin. Eva and Sean spun, turning to run in the other direction. It leaped, jumping over their heads to face them once again. Sean's heart dropped to his belly as he realized they were going to die.

Eva let go of his hand and widened her stance. "Sean, run."

The monster lunged. Eva grabbed its shoulders. It snapped its jaws at her, but the pair was matched in strength and his straining mouth couldn't reach her.

It may have been a monster, but his mother was just as big and just as strong. She held it fast, locked in place while it fought her. Sean looked around for help. But no one paid them any attention. People passed by as if the three of them didn't exist.

"Run, Sean. Go get your father." Eva's face was strained with determination. "This monster is weak. It only looks scary."

He obeyed, running so fast he felt like his chest was going to explode.

When he returned with his father, Eva lay on the ground surrounded by sobbing onlookers. Her throat had been ripped out and shreds of skin, muscle, and bone lay exposed for the world to see. Her eyes were open, and she still had the hard look of determination she had worn when Sean had left her. Blood trickled from her throat and eased towards Sean's flip flops.

Sean and his father left New York that night.

It took five years for Sean to stop waking in the middle of the night with nightmares. It took a year for him to gather the courage to step outside without expecting to see Eva's murderer. It took him another three years to stop seeing Eva's lifeless body every time he closed his eyes. But he never got over the guilt. It was his fault his mother had died. It was his fault his father was alone.

There was no shimmer on Jade, but she still reeked of magic, and he'd seen fey creatures coming and going from her apartment. So, he'd kept his distance from her. But Latreece had outed him, and he'd run, just like he did eight years ago. He was not running anymore. He wasn't going to let Jade hurt Latreece.

Like his mother, he would stand his ground and fight. He was going to get Jade to fix Shemeya and Ashley, then he would get her to leave Latreece alone.

When Sean gathered his nerve and left his apartment, Latreece and Jade were nowhere in sight. The empty playground and basketball court of Vista Apartments slumbered as if it waited for the kids and ballers to return and bring the complex back to life. His father had wanted to leave Vista a few years ago after he'd received a promotion from the hospital, but Sean had pleaded to stay. This was his home. Vista Apartments was the first place he'd felt safe after they fled New York. The people here were his family.

"Andre?" Sean tapped his knuckle on the door. Andre competed with Sean on the basketball court and for girls, but he was the closest thing Sean had to a brother. He'd even tried to hook Andre's mother up with his father. But William had made it clear he wasn't having any of that.

"What do you want?" A voice asked from behind the door.

Sean turned the knob on the unlocked door and tried to walk into the apartment, but Andre pushed from the other side.

"Andre, let me in," Sean insisted. He'd always been allowed in their home anytime he wanted.

"Man, go away. I'm busy," Andre said.

"I need to talk." Sean pushed the door. Andre may have been taller, but Sean was stronger. When the opening was wide enough, he hopped into the apartment.

"Damn!" Andre cursed. He wore a black hoodie, and he kept his head down like he was trying to avoid eye contact.

"Are you sick?" Sean asked. "Why weren't you in school this morning?"

"Yeah, I'm sick. You need to leave before you catch it." Andre backed away and lowered his head.

Sean smelled it: the effervescent scent of magic.

"What's wrong with you?" Sean reached for Andre's hood, but the boy moved away. As if they were on the basketball court, Sean anticipated the dodge and moved in the other direction, parallel with Andre, and pulled off Andre's hood.

As the hood fell, roaches scattered across his face, running away from the light.

Andre yanked the hood back over his head, but Sean couldn't un-see what he just saw.

Sean swallowed the bile and regret rising from his belly. "Damn. Jade got to you, too?" he asked, sick with guilt.

"I'm fine," Andre snapped. "We've just been having roach problems."

"Roaches don't move over a person's face."

Andre's façade cracked, and he wept. "Oh my god. What am I going to do?" he asked.

As Andre cried, bugs ran across his hands and disappeared underneath his hoodie, but Andre didn't seem to feel them. "It just started this morning. I'm scared, Sean. What is my mom gonna say when she sees this?"

Guilt settled into the pit of Sean's stomach. If he'd done something about Jade when he first found out, this whole thing could have been avoided. But shoulda, woulda, couldas wouldn't change the past. He had to do something now.

Sean forced his gaze back to Andre. "Come with me. You're not the only one. She's been messing with Shemeya and Ashley, too. Maybe between the four of us we can fix this."

"I'm not cutting my hair." Shemeya stood in the doorway of her apartment with her hands across her chest, and her dreads tied back in a ponytail.

"That's not why I'm here. Can we come in?" Sean asked, checking to make sure Jade, and especially Latreece, were nowhere near.

Shemeya narrowed her eyes and glared at Andre, who was fidgeting with his head down, acting like he'd just robbed a store. "What's wrong with him?" she asked.

"That's what we need to talk about," Sean said.

She turned up her top lip as if she smelled something bad. "Okay. I guess. But don't try nothin' silly, because I will stab you and him."

"You don't trust me after everything we've been through?"

She furrowed her brow. "I trust you, but I ain't stupid."

When they were safely inside the apartment, Sean made sure to close and lock the door.

"Okay. So, what's going on?" she asked, her suspicion replaced with curiosity.

"Show her," Sean said to Andre.

"No." Andre lowered his head and turned away.

"Show me what?" Shemeya asked.

"She'll understand. She's going through the same thing," Sean insisted.

"I don't see anything crawling on her face?" Andre said, anger straining his voice.

Understanding flashed in Shemeya's eyes. "Jade got to him, too?"

"Yeah," Sean replied, relieved to share the burden. "Can you show him what she did to you first?" Sean asked Shemeya.

Her eyes glittered with excitement. "I've been practicing." She removed her hair tie and ran her hands through her dreads, shaking her head like she was an actress in a damn shampoo commercial.

After a few shakes, her hair rose as if her dreads were attached to helium balloons. As they rose and came towards Sean, the hair fell back, and the five snakes he'd seen a few days ago smiled and hissed in his direction. If she had a few more snakes and wore a white toga, she'd look like the Medusa statue he'd seen as a kid in a Washington DC museum.

Andre's hood had fallen off, and he cowered against the wall. Fear radiated in his eyes as he stared at Shemeya and her snakes.

Shemeya's mouth dropped open. "What the hell is that on your face?" The snakes' hissing increased tenfold; they snapped at him in response to Shemeya's shock.

Sean covered his ears and got between them. "I told you. He's like you. Call off your snakes."

Shemeya stepped back and raised her palms in defense. "I'm not covered in bugs. Gross."

Andre stood straighter, finding his courage all of a sudden. "Girl, I prefer bugs to those damn slimy ass snakes."

She stepped towards Andre, the snakes riled once again. "My snakes are not slimy."

"Well, my bugs are not gross," Andre insisted.

"What the hell?" Sean shouted, unable to believe the conversation he was hearing. "Both of you are crazy. You are covered in bugs. And you have snakes as hair!"

"Calm down," Shemeya snapped. "And don't scream at me in my own home."

"Yeah, man. Calm down." Andre's fear had disappeared, and now he sounded just as prideful as Shemeya.

"Did Jade do that because you said all black girls look like cockroaches?" Shemeya asked Andre.

"Man, you heard about that, too?" Andre asked, rubbing the back of his head.

"That's what you get. You're lucky she didn't turn you into a roach completely."

Sean shook his head. The strangeness of it all sank into his gut and made him feel like he was living through an episode of the *Twilight Zone*. "Will y'all listen? I have to tell you guys something." He needed to tell the truth before he lost his nerve.

Andre laughed, the bugs moved anew on his face. Some even crawled out of his mouth. "You see fairies?" He looked around, mockingly while he sat in Shemeya's living room. "Are there fairies flying around my head?"

"There are roaches crawling in and out of your mouth, and you're laughing at me?" Sean asked, sitting next to Andre.

The day felt too long, and the frustration seeped into his tone.

Andre lifted his hands in defense. "Hey now, I was just joking. Why you gotta start insulting me?"

"Talk, Sean," Shemeya said. "Why do you keep talking about fairies?"

"I can see fey. Monsters."

"So," Andre said.

"We're monsters, and we can see each other." Andre motioned towards Shemeya.

"I'm not a damn monster," Shemeya snapped.

"They're not just monsters," Sean interrupted before they could start arguing again. "They're fey, beings from another realm."

"Another realm?" Shemeya drew each syllable out.

"Let me finish," Sean said.

"Yeah, let him finish," Andre said. His bugs stopped moving, and they focused their hair-thin antennaes in Sean's direction. "Go ahead. I like a good story."

"So Jade is fey?" Shemeya asked after Sean told them about his mother and how she died.

"I'm not sure. I can't see her as a fey. She looks human, but she smells of magic, and she has fey coming in and out of her house."

Shemeya paced back and forth in her living room. Her snakes were lying still on her head, nestling each other. "You see fairies. Your mother saw fairies. You were young and kept looking at the damn things, so your family moved to the middle of Oklahoma. Eight years later, you see fey here, and then we turn into monsters." She stopped mid stride and turned to Sean.

"But you're not sure if she's a fairy?" Shemeya asked.

"Not a hundred percent, but she does things humans aren't supposed to do," Sean answered.

"Like turning me into Medusa and Andre into a bug boy."

"We sound like super villains," Andre said with a hint of humor.

"We would make really cool super villains," Shemeya added, laughing.

"This is not a joke," Sean insisted, confused by their laughter. Were they going crazy on top of everything else? "We have to fix this."

"You're right," Andre said, all humor gone. "If my mom sees me like this, she's gonna trip. They'll hide me away for my entire life, and I'll never get another girl."

"Maybe you can control it," Shemeya said to Andre. "I have mine under control."

"Really?" Andre and his roaches looked at Shemeya expectantly. "How?"

"Relax," Shemeya began. "Think of them as your friends, as an extension of your arm." Shemeya stood tall, and her snakes rose, swaying side-to-side. She shined with triumph and satisfaction. "Now, you try," she said to Andre.

Andre stood and faced Shemeya and Sean. The whites of his teeth and eyes contrasted sharply with the hundreds of brown and black roaches that scampered across his face. He breathed deeply. By the fifth inhale, the bugs began to disperse into Andre's clothes until they were completely out of sight.

"Woohoo! You did it." Shemeya's snakes bounced as she jumped and clapped.

Sean watched them both with a sense of dread. He couldn't let them live the rest of their lives as freaks, even if they seemed to be accepting it. "Come on, guys. We have to come up with a plan."

They were at Sean's house, waiting for Ashley. At first, she had refused when Sean asked her to come over. But as soon as he mentioned Jade, she told him she was on her way, and she hung up before he could tell her anything else.

While they waited, Shemeya sat on Sean's white plastic covered couch watching television.

"When did you get that?" Sean pointed to Shemeya's belly. She'd changed into a pair of jeans and a short t-shirt that revealed a loop-piercing hanging from her belly. The jewelry complemented her dark skin and flat stomach.

"I got it a couple of days ago." She scooted closer to him. "Do you like it?"

Sean licked his lips and swallowed. "Do I like what?"

"My belly ring," she whispered, her breath hot on his ear. He pulled away but found himself staring at her lips. He remembered the night at the party and how soft they felt. He wanted to taste them again. He reached towards her, but then he saw the snakes hovering above his head, and he jumped off the couch.

"It looks nice," he said, remembering the question.

She frowned like she'd just had a piece of candy taken from her. "Whatever." She moved back to the other side of the couch and began flipping through the television stations.

Sean walked to the kitchen to stop himself from thinking about Shemeya and her belly ring. Since he found out about the snakes, he had found himself both repelled and attracted to her.

He entered his kitchen to see roaches scurrying over his trash can, and Andre munching on a discarded apple. "What are you doing?" Sean asked, repulsed.

At the sound of Sean's voice, the roaches scattered and ran under Andre's pants. "I'm sorry. I can't control it. Regular food doesn't taste good anymore."

"Man, get out of my kitchen," Sean said, not bothering to hide his disgust.

Something clung to Ashley. It smelled of magic, and it wavered back and forth in and out of Sean's sight. He made sure to look away from it, focusing instead on Ashley. The thing was wispy, immaterial, and when it decided to focus on something, its eyes grew completely black.

Ashley's hazel eyes had always been the most intriguing thing about her. Now, they no longer held color. Instead, they were murky, as if she had severe cataracts.

Sean didn't expect Ashley to believe anything he said. He had expected to have to show her Shemeya's snakes and Andre's bugs, but when he'd told her about Jade, she cried with relief.

"She cursed me, too," Ashley said, sitting next to Sean, looking weaker by the second. "I knew it. I started getting sick right after she did my hair."

"How sick?" Shemeya asked. She sat near Ashley on the arm of the couch. From the lack of fear on her face, she didn't see the thing clinging to Ashley. If she knew about it, Sean didn't think she would be sitting so close.

"My nose started bleeding," Ashley began. "My head hurts. I pass out at least once a day, and I have no energy. I can't keep any food down."

"Have you talked to her?" Sean asked.

"No, I'm scared. But I have something that might help." She pulled the purse from her lap and took out a book that used a brown paper bag as a cover.

He had no idea if it was a ghost, but spook was the only word he could think of. It left Ashley and floated towards the book. The spook looked from the book to Sean expectantly, like it wanted Sean to take it from her.

Shemeya reached for it, and Sean hit her hand away. "If you got it from her, it can't be any good. You need to get rid of it," he told Ashley.

"Oh, Gawd!" Ashley wailed. Her voice so shrill it sounded like a banshee's death cry. "I tried to get rid of it. I've tried. It keeps coming back. I've thrown it in Lake Hefner, Lake Overholser, and in a landfill. It won't leave me." Her voice climbed in panic, "My baby has been staying with my mom because she's scared of me. And her dad went out for beer a few days ago and hasn't returned since. Please, help me."

111

"That's why we're here." Shemeya patted Ashley on the back, still oblivious to the monster she was a few inches away from touching.

"How are we going to fight a witch, though?" Ashley whined.

"She's not a witch," Sean corrected.

"Fey. Witch. It makes no difference. How can we fight her? We don't have magic," Shemeya said.

"Jade can't go against all of us. All we have to do is tell her she has to make you better, or we'll call the police," Sean said.

"The police would never believe us," Andre leaned against the wall. "And if anyone saw me or Shemeya like this, they'd lock us up."

"She's an unlicensed beautician working out of her home," Ashley said. "And she's always leaving that little boy of hers outside playing by himself."

"I babysit for Coal and letting kids play outside is not a crime," Shemeya said defensively.

"It doesn't matter," Ashley said. "Social services will still take him. They did it to my cousins last year."

"That's not a bad idea," Sean said. "We can threaten to report her to the state."

"But how do we know she won't just kill us?" Ashley asked.

"There's power in numbers, and I don't think she is strong enough to take us all out," Sean said.

Jade beamed when she answered the door and saw Shemeya standing on the other side. "How is it going? I've been wondering why I haven't heard from you."

"Shemeya!" Coal appeared beside his mother. "Are you here to play with me?"

Shemeya gave Coal a hesitant smile. "No, I'm sorry. I have to talk to your mom."

That was the signal. Sean stepped away from the side of the door. Ashley and Andre followed.

When Jade saw them, her smile disappeared. "What's going on?"

"We need to talk to you." Shemeya tried and failed to keep the guilt from her voice.

"Why?" Jade asked, ignoring Shemeya and looking directly at Sean.

"Can we come in, please?" Shemeya asked. "It's important."

"Go outside and play, Coal. This'll only take a few minutes."

Coal slumped his shoulders and walked past the four of them. Once outside, he began kicking a red ball that had been lying in the grass.

When Sean stepped into the apartment, the intense feeling of otherness overpowered his senses. The earthy smells brought the memory of his mother's death crashing back.

He closed his eyes, took a deep breath and gathered his courage. He was in charge. And Jade was nothing compared to the monster who had killed his mother.

He could do this.

"What's going on?" Jade asked, her sharp voice pulling Sean out of his thoughts.

"You need to fix us," Ashley demanded. She looked stronger than she had at Sean's apartment, the hope of a remedy giving her strength.

Jade glared at them all in turn before she asked. "Fix what?"

Ashley pulled a gun out of her purse. "Take this damn curse off me, or I'll kill you."

Sean stepped back, surprised. "Ashley, we never talked about bringing a gun."

Jade never moved. She stared at the weapon as if Ashley were holding a stick. "There is no curse on you," Jade said. "The book you took is warded. All you have to do is return it, and the curse on your back will be gone."

All confidence left Ashley, and her hands shook.

"Did you bring the book?" Sean asked Ashley, anxiously eying the gun. He feared it would go off, and they would all be charged with murder. He didn't think Jade was human, but the police wouldn't know that.

Tears sprung from Ashley's eyes, and she plopped on Jade's couch, looking exhausted. The phantom on her back grinned with triumph. "No, I left it in your house."

Sean took the gun from Ashley, deciding he liked the confidence of having something dangerous between them and Jade, just in case she was more powerful than she appeared. "What about Shemeya?"

Jade furrowed her brow. "What about her?"

Shemeya spoke up. "I have snakes as dreads." Her voice shook as if she was betraying her best friend.

"Really?" Jade glanced upwards, disbelief in her voice. "You look normal to me."

Shemeya shook her head, and the snakes rose, hissing.

"Wow!" Jade said with amusement and awe. "How did that happen?" She lifted her hand towards the snakes. They hissed and moved away. After a moment, they relaxed and leaned into her hand.

Angered by Jade's feigned ignorance, Sean stepped closer.

"What do you mean 'how did this happen'? You did this to her."

"I didn't do this." Jade caressed the snakes once more before she turned to Sean. "I have never seen someone's hair turn into snakes. Besides, Shemeya has never done anything to me. I thought we were friends." She turned from Sean to Shemeya. "Child, you must have some type of magic all your own. I used your essence, a power you already possessed, to give you confidence. Your snakes have nothing to do with me."

"You're lying," Sean gripped the gun tighter. "You're Fey. You're doing all of this. What about Andre?" Sean walked over to Andre, and with his free hand he pulled back Andre's hood. The roaches covering his head scattered.

115

"Hey," Andre said with a weak voice, unable to muster any anger.

A smile touched Jade's lips. "Okay. That is my fault, but I was going to call the roaches off tonight." The tips of her fingers moved across Andre's face as the roaches scurried away. "Damn. I didn't know the spell would take so well." Andre stared at her, his jaw clenched, but he did not pull away. "Do you still believe black women look like cockroaches?"

"No, I told you I was just joking." Andre seethed.

"It was not funny." Her voice held an edge of condemnation, and Andre looked away from Jade as if he'd been burned.

"You." She turned her attention to Sean. "You know what I am?"

"Yes." The gun was heavy in his hands, but fear made him hold it tighter.

"How? I am not using glamour. This is true skin."

"You reek of magic."

"Really? Magic has a smell." She tapped a finger on her lips. "I'll have to fix that."

Jade pointed to Ashley, who sat slumped on the couch as if the last bit of strength had left her. "Get up and get my book. And I'll fix you and bug boy."

"Wait," Sean said. "What about Latreece? What did you give her?"

"You have it in your head that I'm a horrible, evil monster. I'm almost sorry to disappoint you. I gave the girl a harmless human root. It's no worse than any other vegetable. It'll help her gain a few pounds, regulate her cycle, and boost her self-esteem. And it'll do all of this naturally because she believes it will."

The relief Sean felt knowing Latreece would be okay vanished as Jade's front door swung open, and five figures stepped into the apartment. His hands shaking, Sean lowered the gun, his fear overwhelming his earlier confidence.

GALENA

Living is Easy with Eyes Closed. — *John Lennon*

Q ueen Galena phased into the forest of the human realm while birds chirped incessantly, begging to be loved. The late morning sun, which both the human and fey realms shared, beamed weakly through the dense canopy of maple and oak trees. The smell of fresh rain was quickly dissipating with the rising heat. She couldn't hear the footsteps of her two personal guards walking behind her, but she knew they were there. After decades of training and fighting together, they were linked like shadows. Usually, they walked beside her, but today that honor went to her daughter. "Welcome to the human realm, Chalcedony," Queen Galena said.

Chalcedony beamed as she turned in a circle, her red eyes probing the forest. Queen Galena had been hesitant to bring the child, but the girl had begged and pleaded until Galena caved. Madoc, her closest advisor, had counseled against it. He believed Chalcedony was too immature, impulsive, and stubborn. He wanted her left in the fey realm until she'd outgrown those traits. Those habits could get her killed here. But he didn't see that she was also relentlessly determined. After months of questions about humans, human technology, and ceaseless begging, Galena had given in.

"Where are all of the humans, cars, and concrete?" Chalcedony asked as they walked through the trees.

Galena sighed. Perhaps Madoc had been right. "To make sure no human will see us, we phase into a forest. Usually, that means no humans and no human technology."

"Oh. I remember. Sorry." Hearing the agitation in her mother's voice, Chalcedony straightened and her smile disappeared. But wonder, excitement, and anticipation still emanated from her in waves. For all of Galena's training, she couldn't help but share the girl's excitement. If she were honest, she'd been looking forward to her daughter's first trip to the human realm. As a child, Gelena had been just as excited as Chalcedony to visit.

As they left the forest, they saw a short, dark-skinned man fidgeting beside a tan car. From the fear and nervousness Galena smelled radiating from him, she knew he was waiting for her.

"Are you the Fey Queen?" he asked once they were face to face. He glanced at Chalcedony and then to her shadows Mahal and Zanete.

"Who else would I be?" Galena had never been to Oklahoma. She only knew it was in the middle of the United States. The place was far from any portal, but rogue fey often traveled great distances, hoping to remain undetected.

But there was no place safe from her, or the other two queens.

The human bowed, showing her the top of his bald head. "I'm sorry. I had to make sure. My name is William."

"William," Queen Galena drew out his name, wrapping it in magic to compel him to tell her the truth, "if you cannot see us in our true form, why did you call?"

"I can't see past glamour, but I know the signs of," he hesitated, "fey. I have relatives who have suffered from the curse."

The man had just saved his own life. Queen Galena motioned towards the human's car. "Take me to this rogue fey."

The spaciousness of these apartments surprised her. The cities on the east coast of the United States where fey usually tried to hide were filled with humans stacked on top of each other. There was always someone in sight, which made the hunts cumbersome. She always had to plan meticulously. If there were rogue fey in this place, it would be easy to track them down without too many humans getting in the way.

William stopped at a building where a boy kicked a blood red ball against a wall. He was a year or two younger than Chalcedony. He stopped as soon as he saw them. "Wow," he said to their group. "Your ears look funny. You must be here for my momma."

"Is this it?" Queen Galena whispered to William.

"Yeah. Jade. She's his mother," William said. He had been confident on the way here, but when he saw the boy, his hand began to shake.

Queen Galena stared at the boy's ears. His ears were perfectly rounded. There were no scars or nubs to show that they'd been cut to appear human. And he didn't smell of fey. He must have been stolen. She'd encountered lots of fey who had taken human children to help fit in. "What's your name?"

"Coal. Are you looking for my mom?" he asked eagerly. "She already has company right now."

"I'm sure she won't mind some extra visitors. We've traveled far to see her," Queen Galena said. She killed humans who saw through glamour, but he'd have to wait. Right now, she was more curious about his so-called mother.

"This way," William said, leading them towards an apartment door with the number 180 on the front.

"Wait." Coal stared at Chalcedony. "Do you want to play with me? My mom says I have to stay outside when your kind is here. And since you're a kid maybe you should wait out here, too."

Chalcedony stared at the boy with her mouth agape, and Galena knew the last thing Chalcedony wanted was to stay outside. But maybe he had a point. "Stay here, Chalcedony," Queen Galena whispered in her ear. "Make sure he doesn't leave."

Chalcedony frowned, disappointment written in her downturned lips, but she did as she was told and turned towards the boy.

Queen Galena, William, and her shadows continued the few steps to the apartment.

Before they entered, she cast a spell. The words of intense magic would keep anyone from seeing or hearing anything in the apartment. The words didn't matter. It was the power and magic behind them that made most of her spells work.

For the next thirty minutes, any human nearby would see an empty yard and feel an intense desire to be anywhere but here.

Zanete took the lead. She turned the knob and nodded when it turned, unlocked.

They entered the house.

Queen Galena drank in the scene. Magic was everywhere. There must have been some type of barrier protecting the small apartment from the outside because the house was breathing powerful magic from its core. How did her waifs, who were supposed to feel any magic in the human realm, not know about this? How did she not feel it from outside?

There were five people in the room. Two appeared to be human, and she did not know what the other three were. Her senses said they were human, but their appearances told a different story.

"Who lives here?" she asked.

They all pointed to a woman with tightly coiled red hair and freckles. Galena looked to the human who had brought her.

"Yes, that's her. Jade." William's gaze darted back and forth between her and the others in the apartment, his nervousness growing.

"Who are these other people?" she asked William.

"They're just neighborhood kids. I think she's cursed them," he said, with a shaky, expectant voice, staring at the girl with snakes in her hair.

The woman they pointed to was the one who looked the most human. Galena probably would have thought they were liars, only trying to draw attention away from themselves, but Jade grabbed the gun that one of the others had. She pointed it at Galena and pulled the trigger.

Stupid humans and their guns.

If she'd been a typical elf, a gun would have been enough to kill her, but she was a queen. She wielded the magic of a hundred generations of fey. Queen Galena focused her power on the bullet. Using her will, she propelled the flying metal backwards. The redhead dropped to the ground, and the bullet lodged into the wall. Queen Galena phased beside the woman and placed her foot on the woman's neck, instantly cutting off her air supply.

"You obviously know who I am." Queen Galena lightly pressed on the woman's throat. She had to be careful. It didn't take much to crush a windpipe and Queen Galena needed the woman to be able to speak. "Who are you? What are you?"

"I'm human. You can't touch me," Jade said with a brittle, raspy voice while she pushed against Queen Galena's foot.

"Your home is filled with magic. A human yielding true magic is impossible. What are you?" Galena used more force. Jade's eyes grew large and wide with the effort to breathe, and her face flushed blue.

Perhaps she is simply a human, Galena thought. But the smell of magic and power permeated the air. Magic felt foreign and out of place in this world of plastic, concrete and metal. It was obvious that nothing was as it appeared in Jade's home.

After a minute, she released some of the pressure on Jade's throat, and words escaped from the redhead's mouth. "This is not pure magic. I only deal in herbs and natural remedies."

Out of the corner of her eye, Galena saw the abominations move towards the front door. She turned towards them while keeping her foot on Jade. "No one leaves." Knowing her intent, her shadows blocked the door. Queen Galena returned her attention to the oddity before her.

"What are you?" Galena asked once more, her impatience growing.

"I'm human," the woman repeated, gasping for breath.

Queen Galena picked up Jade and spun her around. She covered Jade's lips with her own, and the Jade's eyes widened, this time from shock instead of pain.

Her lips were warm. They tasted of fear, fey, and magic. *She was deliciously not human*, Galena thought as Jade tried her best to escape Queen Galena's grasp. Whatever Jade was, she tasted immensely powerful.

As Queen Galena fed, she became aware of something piercing her skin. Somehow Jade had shifted her fingers into talons, and they were lodged in Galena's shoulders. If she hadn't been feeding, that would have been very painful. But with such a strong source of magic, Galena felt no pain. She felt nothing but ecstasy.

Galena watched as the woman's brown-tinted skin turned pale. Jade's short, kinky hair grew straight and long past her shoulders. Her ears extended and grew pointed. Lastly, her dark brown eyes turned red.

She had the red eyes of fey royalty.

The red of a queen.

Understanding dawned. Jade was not only an elf. She was also a shapeshifter.

Galena knew of only three shapeshifters, and they were all queens. Any other fey, she'd kill for what they'd done here, but she needed to know what and who Jade was.

She released the rogue, and Jade fell to the ground gasping.

Giddy from the magic, Queen Galena counted to five as she brought herself back from the intense high of the stolen magic. She turned to face the others in the room. What in all the realms had Jade been doing? She knew these were humans; but one had hair of snakes; another seemed to be morphing into a cockroach; and another was cursed and wilting, decaying by the second, a phantom sucking away her life.

"Were you experimenting with magic to make other shapeshifters?" Queen Galena asked the rogue.

Jade never looked up or bothered to answer the question. She cowered on the floor, chest heaving as she struggled to breathe. Still something told Queen Galena to fear her.

Always one to listen to her instincts, she kicked the rogue in the stomach and once in the head to make doubly sure she wouldn't get up.

She'd get the answers she needed from Jade later. Now, she had to focus on everyone else in the room. Galena had never seen anything like the living horrors in front of her. Not even in the torture chambers of the weavers.

It was old dangerous magic that had turned these humans into abominations. She stared at them each in turn, using the new wave of power she'd stolen from the rogue to render the atrocities powerless. She'd have to take them to the fey realm and study them. Until then, they'd be lifeless automatons, doing what she willed them to.

All but one.

"What are you? You are not like the rest," Queen Galena asked. The boy who appeared humans. The others huddled behind him as if he were the leader. As if he could protect them.

"I asked you a question. Why are you here?"

"We came here to force Crazy Jade to make us better." He met her eyes with steely defiance. His hands were balled into fists at his sides.

"Us? Is there something wrong with you also?"

"No, there isn't anything wrong with him. This is my son." William stepped between Queen Galena and the boy. "He shouldn't be here."

"This was the family member with the curse?" Galena asked. "Don't lie to me, because I'll smell it."

William's son spoke again, his voice full of hate. "I can't see you, but I see the others for what they are. You must be like her." He sneered at the transformed elf on the floor. "Able to hide behind something more than glamour."

The boy was much taller than his father, but she saw the resemblance.

Galena smiled. She loved unpredictable days. When humans and fey mixed, you never knew what would happen. "For telling me about the rogue, I'll give you a choice. Die or have your sight taken away."

"What do you mean?" the boy's father asked.

"Humans are not allowed to see us. So I repeat. You die, or I blind you."

The boy, to his credit, didn't try to run. "I don't want to die."

"So be it." She touched his eyes. Using her will coupled with magic, she extracted the fluid that helped him see. His teeth gritted against the pain as she pressed harder on his eyes. When she first tried this, most had died. But she had perfected the technique over the years.

She removed her hand.

When he blinked, she saw that his pupils had changed from black to white, telling her that she'd succeeded.

Queen Galena felt a brief pang of guilt when the boy's father began crying, but she reminded herself that she was doing the boy a favor. She usually killed humans who saw past glamour. With that in mind, her guilt vanished, and she faced her shadows. "We are finished here."

"What are you going to do with my friends?" The boy grabbed her arm, staring at nothing.

Constance Burris

"I'm taking them with me. I need to find out what happened to them."

"But they're humans," the boy pleaded.

"Not anymore. I don't know what they are." She removed his hand from her arm. "But don't worry. I'll take good care of them."

CHALCEDONY

"We'll be Friends Forever, won't we, Pooh?" asked Piglet.

"Even longer," Pooh answered.

— *Larry Clemmons*

C halcedony scowled as her mother and the others left her behind.

She wanted to be inside with all the action. She had begged for six months to go on a trip to the human realm and hunt rogue fey, but now instead of hunting, she was babysitting

"What's up? You want to play kickball?" the boy asked. His eyes were dark orbs of light, and Chalcedony wondered how many other humans had eyes so intense.

She sighed deeply, wishing again that she was with her mother. "What is kickball?"

"I kick it to you, and then you kick it back to me."

She'd seen plenty of children playing similar games in the fey realm, but she'd never played. There were never any kids around her home to play with. Well that, and they were all scared of her mother's wrath.

Taking Chalcedony's silence as a yes, he kicked her the ball. She ran towards it and struck it so hard that the ball flew over his head and landed several feet away.

"Not that hard. You have to kick it directly to me," he shouted, running after it.

"My name is Coal. What's yours?" he asked, once he returned with the ball securely in his hand.

"Chalcedony."

"Kal-sa-da-nee." He said it slow like he was etching her name in his memory. After he was satisfied, he'd pronunced it right, he dropped the ball and kicked it.

She returned it, and this time it stayed on the ground. Chalcedony had to fight to keep the joy from showing on her face.

"See. It's easy," he said, triumphantly as if it was his achievement, not hers.

"Are you human?" Chalcedony asked.

Coal ran towards the ball and kicked it hard, but she'd gotten into the groove and stopped it.

He looked at the ball trapped underneath her foot. "I don't know," he answered, gnawing on his bottom lip and looking uncomfortable.

"Why don't you know?" she asked with a mixture of curiosity and confusion. "Is your mother human?" She returned the ball, and as before he stopped it with his foot.

"I'm not supposed to tell anyone this, but you have ears like hers, so I think it's okay." He nudged the ball gently with the tip of his shoe. "Sometimes my mom is normal and she looks like everyone else, and sometimes she looks like you, with white skin and pointy ears."

Chalcedony was about to explain glamour and why his mother could be two different people, when he stopped moving in the middle of a kick.

"What's wrong?" she asked, following his gaze.

The door to the apartment stood open, and Mahal, one of her mother's shadow guards, had an elf with long red hair slung over his shoulder. Her head and torso bounced limply from side-to-side like a dead person as she was carried away.

Coal ran towards Mahal. Before he reached the guard, Zanete pulled him away. "What are you doing with my mom? What's wrong with her?"

Chalcedony felt sorry for the boy as he fought uselessly against the strong arms keeping him from his mother.

Queen Galena moved her hands in Coal's direction and the light, so odd looking in such dark eyes, was suddenly extinguished.

He stood still and motionless.

Chalcedony rushed to her mother's side. "What are you going to do with him?" she asked hurriedly.

"He's a human child who can see through glamour, so I'll have to kill this one."

"Wait," Chalcedony said, grabbing her mother's hand. "Can't he come with us? I never have anyone to play with. All of the other fey are scared they'll hurt me and get in trouble." She knew asking to spare Coal's life meant it would be a long time before she would be allowed back in the human realm, but she could not sit back and let him die. He was the only person she'd ever met who didn't treat her like . . . a princess.

"Please, Momma. Please."

Queen Galena rolled her eyes. "Fine, bring him."

COAL

BOOK ONE OF THE EVERLEAF SERIES

CHAPTER ONE

Coal held the newly forged sword at arm's length. The sentient weapon vibrated in his grasp, urging him to attack, but he tightened his sweaty hands around the leather hilt and ignored the foreign impulses. He had been forging swords and practicing with the completed weapons long enough to know when to attack and when to bide his time and let the fight come to him.

Grigory, the master swordsmith, advanced. Coal parried, stepping aside and swinging his sword with all of the skill he'd gained from the two years of working the forge. Grigory fell to the ground, effortlessly rolling beneath the sword before bouncing back to his feet.

"Is she overwhelming you?" Grigory asked as they faced each other. They had been dueling for the past hour. Sweat dripped from Coal's forehead, back, and arms, but just like every other time they'd dueled, the master swordsmith showed no sign of exertion.

"She's restless." Coal wiped the sweat from his forehead with the back of his hand. "But I'm in contr—"

Grigory rushed forward with an arcing swipe. Coal raised his sword to meet the strike. For a moment, their strengths were equal. His sword vibrated with glee as Coal threatened to overcome Grigory.

Forcing the sword's excitement to the back of his mind, Coal focused all of his strength into his upper body and pushed outward.

Overwhelmed, Grigory leaped back.

During the two years of forging swords and sparring with the master swordsmith, Coal had never had the strength or skill to complete such a move. For an instant, he let himself—and the sword—enjoy their accomplishment.

He was so distracted by his small victory that he almost didn't notice when Grigory spun round, his left leg heading towards Coal's knees. Coal dove away, Grigory's boots just skimming his leg. He rolled over frantically, to find a sword pointed at his neck.

Grigory lowered his blade. "You were distracted."

"I almost had you," Coal said with an intense rush of pride and confidence.

"You did not," Grigory said, scratching the eye patch over his left eye. "You've been slow and lazy all morning."

"But I finally completed the block."

"Not with any speed. You're gaining strength and height, but that's nothing to be proud of. What is the point of winning the bind if you are beheaded a moment?"

Coal let Grigory's words sink in while he caught his breath. "You're right. I've been a little distracted. I'm supposed to meet Princess Chalcedony soon." He glanced at the sun, trying to gauge the time. It hung low in the morning sky, but the springtime rays were much stronger than they were when he'd arrived.

Time for him to go.

Grigory lifted the eyebrow above his remaining eye. The other had been gouged out 200 years ago when he served as a soldier instead of a swordsmith. "How long has it been since you've seen her?"

Coal bit his lip while he pretended to think about the answer he already knew. "Two months."

Grigory took the sword from Coal's hands. It would be presented to Chalcedony on her coronation as queen. Magic reinforced the silver shaft, and its black leather hilt emanated heat and welcomed touch. By far, it was the best sword they'd forged.

"Before you go, I have something to ask you." Grigory kept his shoulder-length black hair tied in a low ponytail and his beard trimmed. Both elven and dwarf blood coursed through his veins. As the only known half-breed of his kind, he had the height of an elf and the thick, muscular build of a dwarf.

"What is it?" Coal asked. The way Grigory spoke made Coal wonder if he'd done something wrong, besides being too distracted during the fight.

"I'm getting older," Grigory said. "I need to choose a full-time apprentice, and it needs to be soon. Do you want the position?"

Coal's breath caught in his throat. Had he heard right? "I thought I was just helping out until you found a full-time apprentice?"

"Well, you've passed the two-year audition, and now I'm offering you the job."

"But humans can't do magic." It was one of the first things Coal had learned when he'd arrived in the fey realm eleven years ago. Powerful swords were impossible to make without magic. It made the swords stronger, lighter, and prevented someone else from using it.

"I'm half dwarf and half elf," Grigory said. "For years, my master refused to teach me because he didn't think a half-breed could make a great sword. Now, I am the best swordsmith in Everleaf. It's what's inside that makes a good swordsmith. I believe you could be one of the greats."

Coal had been coming to the forge almost every day for two years, but he was allowed to come and go as he pleased. With a full apprenticeship, he'd eat, breathe, and sleep smithing. He'd have to move out of his home.

"I don't know, Grigory. I need time to think about it." Coal enjoyed forging swords. He especially loved practicing with them, ensuring they would endure battle, but he didn't know if he wanted to make it his life's work.

"Your childhood friend is soon to be queen. She will not have time, or tolerance, for a lovesick human."

Coal was hurt, but not surprised by Grigory's words. No one said anything to his face, but he heard the servants and soldiers gossiping about him and Princess Chalcedony when they thought he wasn't listening. "You're right, but give me time. It's not easy choosing one life over another."

Grigory's eye softened. "You and the future queen still have much growing to do. Decide soon. I won't wait long."

Coal glanced back towards the rising sun. "It's time for me to go."

Grigory waved his hand as if to swat a fly, before he turned back to the forge.

Bees and butterflies as big as his hands buzzed around Coal's ankles while he walked through a meadow of red, yellow, and blue wildflowers that separated the forge from his home. He felt guilty for not accepting Grigory's offer, but as he approached his home, the guilt faded and a smile grew across his face. He lived in Legacy, the biggest tree in the fey realm, with his best friend Princess Chalcedony, her staff, and a handful of ambassadors from every part of the realm.

At 850-feet tall and ten times as wide as Grigory's modest home, Legacy seemed to be larger than life. Residing inside of a living, sentient thing, made him feel like he was a part of something remarkable. The moment he saw it years ago, Coal knew he'd made it home.

"Legacy." Coal touched the coarse bark of the oak tree and instantly felt the life thrumming inside it. "Is Chalcedony back?"

There are so many here today. How am I supposed to keep track of any one person? Legacy said, its voice full of annoyance. Legacy was neither male nor female, but its voice sounded female nonetheless.

"Come on, Legacy. Is she in her room?"

The tree gave an exaggerated sigh as the breeze rustled its leaves. *When last I bothered to listen, she was in her office and she was asking for you.*

"Thanks," Coal said, relieved to hear that Princess Chalcedony had returned. He removed his hand and approached the two female sentries guarding Legacy's main entrance. Like all of Everleaf's elven soldiers, they wore a dark green shirt with black sleeves and black pants.

"Where are you going?" asked the taller of the two, who had light green eyes. She stepped in his way, blocking the door. "The servant's entrance is around the back."

"I'm not a servant." Coal held the sentry's gaze. He'd never seen these two before, but he'd done this dance countless times over the years. He was a human in a world where humans were mostly banned and thought of as violent, ignorant, and greedy. His stomach churned as he faced the sentry, but he stood his ground. If he showed fear, it only made the taunting worse.

"No." The other sentry stood a head shorter than her partner, but where the other was slender, she was more muscular. "He's not a servant. He's just human trash."

He swallowed. "Let me through."

"Or what?" The taller sentry placed a hand on her sword. "You'll tell the princess I was picking on you?"

"I don't need the princess to protect me," he snapped. "I can take care of myself."

"Calm down, Sophia," the shorter sentry said. "Let him through. Today will be his last day here anyway."

"What are you talking about?" Coal narrowed his eyes, his pulse quickened. This was not part of the usual bullying.

"Don't worry about it," the sentry said, pulling the green-eyed sentry away from Coal. "I apologize for my partner. Her great-great something or other died in the human and fey wars."

"Well …" Coal deepened his voice, his attitude bolstered by the change in her tone. "Don't let it happen again."

"Of course not." The shorter sentry bowed. "Again, I apologize."

Coal walked past the sentries and through the entrance, deciding they had only been trying to scare him. But why would she say it was his last day here?

Once he entered the grand hall separating the entranceway from Chalcedony's offices, he understood why Legacy sounded upset. Staff bringing food from the kitchen and filling mugs with milk, juices, and mead crowded the hall with bustling energy. Almost every race of fey had gathered in the hall—or at least every race of fey that ventured out in the daytime—elves, giants, dwarves, satyrs, nymphs, and even a few trolls.

Coal touched the wall and said to Legacy, "The ambassadors aren't supposed to be here until tomorrow." It had been quiet for the past three weeks. However, now that Chalcedony had returned from the human realm, fey from every corner of Everleaf came to meet with her.

Obviously, they decided to come early, Legacy said.

Disappointed, Coal broke the connection with the tree. Before she'd left on her last training trip, Chalcedony had said she had something special planned for the two of them. Her duties came first, though. If she had to work, she wouldn't have time for him.

He peered into the crowd, searching for the path of least resistance. Finding it, he lowered his head, stepped out of the safety of the entranceway, and walked into the congested gathering. The smell of goat sausage and fried eggs wafted towards him, making his stomach rumble with hunger. He'd awakened before the kitchen staff, and only had time to eat an apple before he'd left for Grigory's.

"Did you really think you were going to walk by me without speaking?" A deep voice said behind him. Coal twisted round and looked up into the gray eyes of the eight-foot tall, tawny-skinned giant named Octavius.

"Soon..." Octavius winked one of his gray eyes at Coal, "I hear you'll be reigning next to Chalcedony."

"Princess Chalcedony and I are only friends." Coal lost his appetite. Humans were considered weak. If Chalcedony took on a human mate, she would be considered weak also.

The day had started full of promise. He'd looked forward to spending time with Chalcedony, but his plans were quickly unraveling. With the giants and dwarves here, it would be impossible for her to slip away. And, for the second time today, someone had reminded him he didn't belong.

"Don't look so insulted." Octavius grabbed Coal's shoulder. "My great-great-grandmother was human. I'd consider it an honor to have a human reigning beside the queenling."

"Hmph, that would never happen," said Ambassador Eli. The dwarf seemed to have appeared out of nowhere, his head a mass of dark curls. "Humans are exiled for a reason. They are violent, greedy, and, above all, parasitic." He stared at Coal with light blue eyes and sneered.

Octavius shook his head and clicked his tongue. "No, giants are humans, only taller. That's why we can't wield magic. And there is nothing extraordinarily violent or parasitic about us."

"Stop it with the myths. That's like saying dwarves are human, only shorter," Ambassador Eli said. "If your brother heard you speak like that, he'd have you whipped."

The temptation to stay and listen to Octavius and Ambassador Eli argue nearly overpowered him, but the idea of seeing Chalcedony pulled much stronger. They were too busy debating the differences between humans and giants to notice Coal slip away.

Coal stood outside of Chalcedony's thick wooden door and straightened his brown pants and the white shirt he wore underneath his green jerkin. He ran a hand over his braids and noticed one of them had unraveled. He cursed under his breath as he re-braided his kinky textured hair as fast as he could before he knocked on the door.

"Who is it?" asked a gruff voice from inside the room. It was Chalcedony's royal advisor, Madoc. Coal was convinced that Madoc's primary goal in life involved making Coal miserable.

"It's me," Coal said in his most formal voice. "Legacy told me that Chalcedony is looking for me."

The door opened, and Princess Chalcedony stood on the other side. "Legacy's right. I am looking for you." She wore a black sleeveless shirt and matching pants that were only a few shades darker than her brown skin.

Coal bowed, bending low at the waist while happiness surged in his chest at the sight of his oldest friend.

"How can I help you, Princess?" he asked.

"Come in." She stepped back from the door, her muscular arms flexing as she motioned for him to step into the room. "Since when do you bow, or call me princess?"

Since last week, when Madoc lectured me for ten minutes about properly addressing a future queen, Coal wanted to say, but instead, he kept quiet. The less he said, the less Madoc could use against him when Chalcedony left.

Once he stepped in the room, he saw there were three other fey sitting around the table in Chalcedony's office. Madoc sat closest to the door, scribbling on a sheet of paper. He scoffed at Coal before he turned towards the stack of papers.

"If I am no longer needed, I'll be retiring to my room," said Binti, the female waif who had been sitting at the end of the table. She had a jumbled network of tiny blue veins that showed underneath her pale translucent skin. As she stood up from the table, the loose pink dress she wore buckled around knobby knees before she pulled it down.

Binti and her twin brother acted as a tether between the two realms. If a rogue fey used magic in the human realm, her brother felt it. Through the link the siblings shared, her brother would let Binti know. Then, Binti would alert Chalcedony in the fey realm.

"Go ahead," Princess Chalcedony said. "Thanks for your help."

Binti nodded briefly at Chalcedony as she walked away from the table and towards the door. Coal shivered as she passed. The waif lowered the temperature of any room by five degrees just by her presence. They were rumored to be children of reapers sent into the physical world to live until they replaced their parents as harvesters of souls.

Motion next to Chalcedony caught his attention. He was drawn to the blonde, blue-eyed elf standing next to Chalcedony.

Tetrick.

Chalcedony had spent the past two years with the high-born elf. He was appointed by his mother, Queen Tasla, to teach Chalcedony how to patrol her part of the human realm for fey who were there illegally. "Are you sure you wouldn't like me to escort you, Princess?" Tetrick asked.

As usual, the royal elf paid Coal no attention. Coal didn't know if it was better to be ignored and made to feel like he wasn't worth a second thought, or to be constantly ridiculed and belittled like Madoc treated him.

"No, thank you, Tetrick," Chalcedony answered.

"You should let him escort you," Madoc said with a tone that suggested it was more of an order than a choice.

"No," Chalcedony said with such intensity that her long, sharp incisors were visible. "But thank you anyway," she said to Tetrick, her temper back under control.

"Very well, Princess." Tetrick bowed, and then the elf disappeared as if he'd never been there.

"You should have let him take you," Madoc said.

11

"Take you where?" Coal asked. "I thought we had plans for today."

"We do." Chalcedony's red eyes were wide with joy. "It's a surprise. But first, go get your clothes. Then, I'll meet you upstairs in my room."

"What clothes?" Coal asked, confused. She'd changed from all business to playful so quickly it took Coal a moment to adjust.

"The ones you brought back with you from the human realm."

Coal hesitated. He was five the last time he'd worn those clothes. "Why?"

"You should not question a princess's orders," Madoc said.

Chalcedony huffed and turned to Madoc.

"You're dismissed, Madoc," Chalcedony ordered.

Madoc shot Coal a hateful look before he bowed towards Princess Chalcedony and left the room.

"Don't worry about him. He's in a bad mood."

"He's been in a bad mood for eleven years," Coal said. "I think it's safe to say he just really hates me."

"He doesn't hate you. He treats you just like he treats everybody else."

"Really?" Coal asked with a raised eyebrow.

"Okay, he may dislike you a little bit. Go, and meet me upstairs."

"But—" he began.

"No more questions or you'll spoil the surprise. Just go get them." Her voice was full of joy and mischief. He'd missed it. He'd missed her.

Coal bit his lip, stifling his next question before he left the room.

What could she possibly want with his human clothes? They were all he had that proved where he'd come from, but he hadn't touched or thought about them in years.

Coal stood at Chalcedony's bedroom door a few minutes later, holding a ragged shirt and a pair of pants.

The door stood open, but the room seemed empty until Chalcedony stepped from behind her dressing screen. He almost dropped his bundle when he saw her wearing a pair of blue pants and a yellow shirt. Human clothes.

"What are you wearing? How did you get those?" he asked.

"Jeans and a T-shirt, the items you have in your hands, are very common clothes in the human realm."

"But why are you wearing them?" he asked.

"It's a surprise. Give me yours, and I'll fix them for you."

She took his clothes, placed them on her bed and whispered over them. As she spoke, the holes in the shirt became smaller until they disappeared. The material stretched, becoming longer and wider. She worked the same magic with his pants.

"Wow, you could be a tailor. That'll come in handy if the giants do decide to attack the dwarves."

"Ha ha." Chalcedony smiled in triumph. "Tetrick taught me this two days ago. I'm discovering more abilities the closer I get to my coronation."

He'd always been jealous of Chalcedony's ability to wield magic. Over the years, he'd gotten much better at hiding his envy, but still, every time he saw Tetrick and Chalcedony together, the jealousy and longing returned. Tetrick was strong, powerful, and able to phase in and out of most places anytime he wanted. He was everything Coal wasn't.

"Fine, you can lengthen clothes, but why do we need to wear them?" Coal asked.

"Stop asking questions and relax. I promise you won't be disappointed."

She waved her hand and an invisible force pushed him backward. She'd learned to move things years ago, but it wasn't until recently, that she'd moved anything heavier than a sheet of paper.

"Okay, okay. I won't ask any more questions. I can walk the rest of the way myself."

"Thank you." She lowered her hand, and the force disappeared from his chest. "Be careful back there. I don't want you ending up somewhere you shouldn't."

Reluctantly, but of his own free will, he walked behind the screen with his clothes.

A wave of nostalgia washed over Coal as he remembered the last time he'd ducked behind the screen. It served as Chalcedony's secret portal and her escape route if Legacy was ever invaded, which hadn't happened in over one hundred years. It was one of the best kept secrets in Everleaf. As children, they would travel through the screen pretending to hunt for treasure in the forest while everyone slept.

"So, what do you think?" Coal walked out from behind the screen. He didn't like the feel of the stiff fabric against his skin, but the clothes fit.

She stared, eyes narrowed.

"Did I put them on right?" he asked, feeling self-conscious under her intense gaze.

"You look fine." She smiled. "You look really good, actually."

"Um, thanks." If she liked them, he decided, they couldn't be all bad. "So are you going to tell me why we're dressed like this?"

"Nope." She wrapped a black cloak around her lean shoulders and then handed him an extra one lying on her bed. "Wrap up. I don't want anyone asking too many questions."

Coal followed her out of the room while he tried to hide his excitement and curiosity. His joy disappeared when he saw Madoc at the bottom of the stairs talking to Ambassador Eli. He turned when he saw Chalcedony and Coal.

"You're not taking your shadows?" Madoc asked, cocking his bushy black and gray eyebrow.

"I know how to protect myself."

"Your pride will get you killed. Take your shadows. I'm sure they would appreciate the exercise."

She rolled her eyes. "No. You have to start trusting me."

"Traipsing through the human realm without your shadows is not something a queen would do."

"We're going to the human realm?" Coal blurted.

Constance Burris

"Damn it, Madoc!" Chalcedony exclaimed. "I told you it was a surprise."

Madoc shrugged. "Take your shadows."

Chalcedony answered with a sneer before she stormed out of Legacy.

Coal followed behind Chalcedony while his mind raced. She chattered away, but he couldn't focus. Several moments passed before he asked, "Why didn't you tell me we were going to the human realm?"

"It was a surprise. Surprise!" Chalcedony wore a mischievous grin that made her red eyes sparkle.

In any other situation, Chalcedony's good mood would have been contagious, but he'd been in the fey realm since he was five, and he'd never left Everleaf. He didn't know whether to be scared or excited.

"Why are we going? I've never asked to go there." The fact that Madoc had not argued about Chalcedony taking him worried him. If he knew anything about the elf, it was that he hated Coal. Most especially, Madoc hated Chalcedony to be seen with Coal outside of Legacy. His disapproval had grown more venomous over the past year.

"Are you going to leave me there?" he asked, recalling what the sentries had said.

Chalcedony stopped and faced Coal. "Why would you think that?"

"You didn't answer my question." His heart raced while he waited for a response.

"More and more of my work is there. It's so different. Human tech can be destructive, but it's amazing. Every time I go there I think of you, and I wish you could see it. That's why we're going."

"What about Madoc?"

"Don't worry about him. Do you really think I'd just leave you in the human realm without telling you?"

"No, I don't. It's just—"

"Coal, I've been tracking rogue fey in the human realm and dealing with serious situations for three weeks," she said with desperation in her voice. "I want to have fun. I swear that is the only reason we're going. I swear on my mother's sword."

She held his gaze.

"How are we going to the human realm without Tetrick? Don't you need him to phase us there?"

Chalcedony shrugged and continued walking. "No, we don't need Tetrick."

"Are we taking the dragons?" Coal asked, his curiosity piquing.

"No, we're not flying. We're taking the horses most of the way."

"You're not going to tell me, are you?" Coal asked as they entered the stable.

"Nope."

He smirked. "I didn't think so."

"Just relax," Chalcedony said. "You'll have fun. I promise."

"Are you really going to let them go to the human realm alone?" Ambassador Eli asked Madoc, once Chalcedony and Coal had left.

"She may only be seventeen, but she's smart and one of the strongest in her line. I doubt anyone can hurt her, except for a queen."

"Are you sure you're not overestimating her?" Ambassador Eli asked.

"I may be, but there is only so much I can do." Madoc faced the dwarf. Many dwarven ambassadors had passed through Legacy, and everyone had hated the bureaucratic process, except for Ambassador Eli. To Madoc's surprise, the dwarf seemed just as concerned for Everleaf as he was for protecting his people's fortunes and trade routes.

Ambassador Eli stroked his chin with a short, hairy finger. The dwarf had never worked in the mines so he was slim, instead of bulky and muscular. "I've been hesitant to bring this up, but you should know that most fey in Everleaf have begun to talk about the queenling and her human boy. There are rumors he is destined to become her lover and rule beside her."

"I am well aware of the rumors, but that will never happen."

"What are your plans for him? I expected you to have gotten rid of him long before now."

"Chalcedony is supposed to leave the boy in the human realm while they're there."

Ambassador Eli exhaled. "That's a relief."

Madoc turned back towards the window. Chalcedony and the boy were on horseback, leaving through the gates. "But she lied to me. She is not going to leave him there. She is still too attached to him."

"Then, you need to get rid of him," Ambassador Eli said, his voice lifting.

Madoc watched them until they disappeared from sight. "I can't. The boy will play a significant role in Princess Chalcedony becoming a formidable queen."

"How can you be so sure?" Ambassador Eli asked, his tone full of doubt.

"I had a few truthsayers look into it. They all said the same thing. He's meant to stay until he decides to leave on his own."

The dwarf scowled. "Isn't it your job to make her a great queen?"

"Like I said, I can only do so much. I've shown her the best and the worst duties of being a queen, yet she remains a child. Her mother and grandmother ..." Madoc hesitated, searching for the correct phrase, "had lost their innocence by her age. She is too happy, and it's all tied to the boy. Once he's gone, she'll lose her innocence. Besides, I can't kill him without her suspecting. She is young but intuitive. Out of resentment, she may hurt Everleaf. But if the thing she loves leaves on its own, then that is a different game altogether."

"The boy obviously worships her. He'll never leave without coercion."

"Ambassador Eli, I've been doing this for centuries. You have my word. The prophets have reassured me he won't be around much longer."

CHAPTER TWO

O n horseback, Coal followed Chalcedony away from Legacy, through the town square and into the royal forest. After a few miles, they came upon a lake.

"We can leave the horses here. We have to walk the rest of the way." She bent down and put her hands in the water. "Remember this place?"

"Yeah." The sound of waves falling onto the shore mingled with the chirping of the birds and created a melody, making Coal feel like they were the only people left in the world. "We used to get in so much trouble for using your portal to come here to swim."

"Well, we're a little bit ahead of schedule. Do you want to go swimming?"

"We didn't bring any swim clothes."

She gave Coal a wicked grin. "Never stopped us before."

"That was a long time ago." Coal glanced nervously at Chalcedony's chest before he quickly averted his eyes. "We've changed since then."

Chalcedony tilted her head to the side. "We haven't changed that much."

She walked towards the lake and took off her clothes. At least she was wearing underwear. "You're trying to get me killed, aren't you? What if Madoc is watching?"

"Don't worry about Madoc. He promised he'd let me do anything I wanted today. And right now, this is what I want to do."

It had been a while since he'd been swimming, Coal thought, as he stripped down to his underclothes and followed her into the water.

After being picked up and thrown into the water more times than she counted, Chalcedony ran out of the lake and sat on the grass. It had been a while since she'd done anything merely for fun, and she was glad Coal had warmed up to the idea of going to the human realm. The rift that had been growing between them over the past few months had finally closed.

Coal left the lake and sprinted towards her. She was seventeen, one year older than Coal, and until recently, she'd always towered over him. Her growth had slowed, and she would look this way for the next fifty years. But Coal continued to grow, and surprisingly, he'd caught up to her.

His ebony skin glistened in the midmorning sun as he stood above her. "You give up?" He laughed, one dimple forming on each cheek.

Madoc's Rule Number Eight: Never Admit Defeat. So, she changed the subject. "One of your braids has come undone." Chalcedony sat up and patted her lap. "Come here. I'll re-braid it."

He appeared as if he was going to refuse, but sat down and laid his damp head on her lap anyway. She undid the rest of the braid before passing her fingers through his thick hair to remove any kinks. She grabbed a small section and separated it into three before she began. "It took you forever and a day to learn how to braid. You were the worst student," Chalcedony said as she worked.

"I didn't want to learn. I liked it better when you did it."

"You have gotten better, though."

"I didn't have a choice. You've been too busy to do it," Coal said.

"Madoc thinks it's beneath me to braid my own hair. He most definitely didn't like it when I braided yours."

Coal tensed beneath her fingers at the mention of Madoc, so she changed the subject. "I love how your hair makes a halo around your head. For years, I tried to get my hair to match yours. But it's only darker, not curlier."

"Mmm," he murmured, sounding content and halfway asleep.

She couldn't blame him for being suspicious about this trip. He'd been correct. She was supposed to leave him in the human realm. Agreeing to leave Coal behind was the only way she could get Madoc's approval to bring him along with her. Her coronation was in two weeks, and she needed to relax. Coal was the only person she relaxed with because he was the only person who didn't expect her to be perfect. Lying to her advisor wasn't something she did often, but there was only so much arguing she could do.

Coal's even breathing told her he'd dozed off. She'd forgotten how having his hair braided lulled him to sleep—once she'd learned how to avoid painful tangles.

She bent down and whispered in his ear. "I'm finished, Coal."

He turned his head, but he didn't open his eyes. She placed her hand on his forehead and studied his delicate lips, wondering if they were as soft as they seemed. She forced the thought out of her head and stood, causing Coal's head to drop from her lap and fall onto the ground.

"Ouch." He patted the side of his head. "What's wrong?"

"I'm sorry." Chalcedony staggered towards her clothes before she dressed. "We need to go. It's getting late."

Kissing Coal was the last thing she needed to be thinking about. She stared ahead, avoiding Coal's gaze. *Everything's complicated enough.*

"What's wrong, Chaley?" Coal asked. Her relaxed, playful mood had vanished. What had happened while he slept? What had startled her?

"Nothing's wrong," Chalcedony insisted. "We just need to hurry."

"Which way?" Coal asked, happy to be off the horse and traveling by foot. His butt and inner thighs were beginning to chafe from the saddle.

Chalcedony pointed to a bridge about a mile away through a small opening between the trees. "It's just over the bridge. I'll race you."

She sprinted away before he answered. Relieved she had cheered up, Coal didn't think to run after her until she had already left.

Halfway to the bridge, his legs burned and begged for him to stop. But instead of slowing, his pride pushed him faster and closer to Chalcedony. She twisted her head and grimaced when she saw him nearing. Chalcedony hated to lose. Elves were natural runners and predators, unlike humans, but he'd been running with Chalcedony and other elves for as long as he'd been here. He'd never won, but it never stopped him from trying.

He broke through the trees and into a clearing. The bridge was only a few feet away. With fewer trees, he was able to run fast enough to pass Chalcedony.

Looking to the side, he saw she was half a step behind him. He glanced back towards the bridge, just before colliding into it.

Chalcedony was on the bridge a fraction of a second later.

"I beat you," he gasped. "For the first time, I beat you."

"You nearly killed yourself trying to do it." She stood next to him, steady and calm. A thin layer of sweat prickled the skin above her top lip, but she wasn't breathing nearly as hard as him.

"I still beat you."

Chalcedony stepped behind him with a knife at his throat before he thought to move or defend himself.

"If we were fighting, you would have won a battle but lost the war. You no longer have any strength to combat me." The metal was cold and sharp against his neck.

Coal sobered, his breath finally under control. "Is that what you think?"

The knife pricked his skin. "Yes."

He grabbed Chalcedony's wrist and twisted, the knife fell to the ground. Then he pushed her onto the grass. "Hasn't Tetrick taught you not to underestimate your enemy?" he asked, standing above her, feeling cocky and triumphant. Chalcedony swung her legs around, sweeping Coal's feet out from under him and sending him crashing onto his back beside her. She rolled onto him, laughing and straddling him with her knees. Her long, dark hair hung over the side of her face.

"Are we enemies?"

"Madoc says everyone is your enemy," Coal answered.

"Is he right?" she asked. "Are you my enemy?"

Coal lifted himself onto his elbows and gazed into her eyes. "Chaley, I would die for you."

She bent down and touched her lips to his. He tasted salty, but the kiss was sweet, and it awakened a hunger that had been brewing for longer than she wanted to acknowledge.

CHAPTER THREE

One kiss couldn't hurt, right? Chalcedony thought, but then, she lost herself in the sensation.

Coal's hand brushed through her hair and sending tingles through her body.

"Princess!" someone shouted from behind. Chalcedony leaped off Coal. A royal guard stood a few feet away with his sword drawn.

"Are you okay, Princess?" the guard asked, looking from Chalcedony to Coal, and back again.

Bren, she remembered. One of Madoc's personal lackeys. He had ash-blonde hair with tawny-colored skin. His face was twisted in disgust and anger emanated from his pitch-black eyes.

Coal stepped slowly in front of Chalcedony. She wanted to tell him to stop. Bren was more likely to hurt Coal than her, but she didn't want to take her focus away from the guard. She felt for the hilt of the knife she hid underneath her shirt. "What are you doing here?" she asked, looking over Coal's shoulder.

"I was sent to patrol the forest." His hands shook, but he never lowered his sword.

"Are you going to attack me?" she asked with a haughty toss of her hair, hoping to draw his attention away from Coal. Bren flicked his gaze towards his weapon before he lowered it.

"I'm sorry, Princess. Of course, I would never hurt you."

Chalcedony relaxed, released the knife, and stepped out from behind Coal. "Since when do we patrol the forest?" she asked.

This forest hid the door to the human realm, but it was not guarded. Only a select few were supposed to know it existed. Patrolling would only attract attention. Instead, an invisible barrier that prevented anyone from entering without permission protected the forest.

"Um," Bren stuttered, his eyes lowered.

"Madoc sent you, didn't he?"

"He … um, I was sent to patrol the door," Bren answered. She closed the space between the two of them.

"Look at me," she ordered. He met her gaze. "Are you lying to me?"

"No, Princess. I was assigned to patrol the forest today. I didn't know you would be here."

She studied him, searching for a lie. She was not a mind reader, but Tetrick had taught her to look past a fey's surface to recognize emotions and truth. Chalcedony saw fear, embarrassment, and disappointment, but there was no indication of a lie. Perhaps Madoc had set him up.

"Leave my forest before I have you banished for spying on me," Chalcedony ordered.

"Princess, I'm sorry. I swear I didn't know you would be here," Bren said, shaking.

"Leave now!"

"Yes, Princess."

He placed his sword in its sheath and stalked away. Once Bren disappeared between the trees, she walked towards the bridge.

"Are you alright?" Coal reached for her arm, but she flinched and moved away.

If she wanted Coal to live, she could never let him touch her again.

Coal followed her over the bridge. "Shouldn't we talk about what happened?"

"No. I shouldn't have done that."

He was about to argue with her, but everything was different, wrong. The air became denser, making it harder for Coal to breathe. The trees, the grass, and even the sun were less vivid. It was as if he were looking through a smudged window.

"Chaley, where are we?"

Chalcedony met his gaze. "We're in the human realm."

"I didn't see any door."

She placed her hands on her hips. "If it could be seen, everyone would know where it was."

He turned in a slow circle, drinking in all he saw. The tree's brown bark was dull and washed out. The green leaves were watered down and muted. The grass cracked and moaned underneath his feet as if it were dying of thirst.

He had never stopped to listen to the everyday sounds of life; they'd always been in the background. But the singing and harmony of the forest had disappeared. This terrible silence made him feel as if something were missing.

The human realm, Coal decided, was a weak, lifeless version of the fey realm.

"Chalcedony, stop. I don't understand. How did we get here?"

She frowned, gazing into Coal's eyes as if deciding something. "Few fey or humans know this. You have to keep it secret."

"By now, you know you can trust me," Coal said.

She scanned the forest as if she were scared someone would overhear her. Satisfied they were alone, she said, "During the war, humans and fey decided to separate themselves so we couldn't destroy each other."

"I'm not stupid. I know that part." His anxiousness over the new environment was giving away to agitation.

"They also created portals to connect the two realms, because, in spite of all the war and death, complete separation seemed unfathomable. Also, giants are humans. Every now and then, a giant will have a normal human child, and they wanted to be able to take those children to the human realm if they needed to."

"Ambassador Eli said giants weren't humans."

"Giants used to give birth to humans on a normal basis, but now that humans and giants don't interact as much, it's rare."

"Why haven't I heard of the portal before?"

"Because if everyone knew, the human realm would be overrun with rogue fey," Chalcedony said.

He decided on another random question. "Why does the air smell so different?"

"Their technology pollutes the air." Chalcedony walked through the forest.

The ground was littered with broken tree branches that snapped underneath her feet. Coal marveled. He was in the human realm, his birthplace. Despite his curiosity and excitement, the image of the two of them kissing kept replaying in his mind. As he followed behind her, he wondered when it would happen again.

"Wait." She stopped so abruptly that he almost bumped into her.

She pulled a pouch from the pocket of her pants, placed her hand inside of it. Her fingers came out of the bag covered in a multi-hued powder. She recited a few words before she placed it in her mouth. Slowly, her long, sharp canine teeth widened and shortened. They lost their edge and became flat. Her slim pointed ears curved. Her large red eyes dimmed and turned black. She had changed into a human.

For a moment, Coal did not recognize the person standing in front of him. His vision adjusted as if it was adapting to the dark, and he saw past the illusion. She had swallowed glamour. Humans would look at Chalcedony and see the false image. For him, it was transparent, merely an overlay, barely hiding her true features.

"I'll be glad when I can change my teeth and ears. Tetrick says I should be able to do it soon. Then I won't have to use glamour every time I come here. Do I look human enough?" she asked.

"Yes," he answered. "But it's not as if I've seen many."

"Oh, right." Chalcedony rubbed the back of her neck. "Well, let's go look at some humans." She held out her hand. "We haven't gotten to the fun part yet."

He stared at her hand for a moment before he grabbed it and let her pull him out of the forest.

Cars. He remembered them from his childhood.

Red, yellow, blue, green, black. They sped by one after the other, leaving metallic fumes in their wake. Slowly he remembered other things, forgotten memories of concrete, laughing and running, and a woman's touch—soft and tender.

"Stay close." Chalcedony's voice pulled him out of his thoughts. "Are you okay?" she asked, staring at him intently.

He tried to put what he saw into words, but the memories were gone just as quickly as they'd appeared. "I'm fine." He looked around in an attempt to anchor himself. They were waiting for what he knew was a streetlight.

"Where are we going?" he asked.

"A coffee shop," Chalcedony said. "It's not far."

When the cars stopped, he followed Chalcedony across the street. As they walked, Coal studied the people's faces.

Most avoided eye contact, but some stared directly at him and smiled.

"We're here." She stopped at a building with a sign that read "Ground Beans." "It's a coffee shop. I figured this would be a nice place to sit and relax."

Coal shrugged, noting the hesitation in her voice. "This is your adventure. I'm just along for the ride."

She stood a little straighter, and he followed her into the shop. Coal sat in one of the wooden chairs next to a window while Chalcedony ordered. The noonday sun beamed through the windows and the smell of coffee and baked bread permeated the air. Chalcedony brought him coffee and a cream-filled pastry. For the second time that day, he was reminded how he hadn't had breakfast. He ate the pastry in three quick bites. He'd expected for it to be bland, like the dull colors of the human realm, but it tasted sweet and flavorful.

"I never get to do anything like this." Chalcedony bit into her pastry, chewed, and then swallowed. "I hunt rogue fey and then, we immediately go back home." She leaned back and smiled as the sunlight danced on her face.

"Why did you bring me here?" he asked.

Chalcedony stared out of the window at the crowded street. "I wanted to show you this. Most of the people here are college students. Look at how easy they live and how happy they are. They're a few years older than us, but they have no responsibilities. Their only job is to go to school. That's it."

Coal noticed half of the people in the shop had devices in front of their faces and wires connected to their ears. They didn't look happy. They spoke in high, grating voices, a sharp contrast to the husky and almost guttural sounds he had grown used to in the fey realm.

"I dream about running away and living here—maybe just the two of us," Chalcedony added.

"Why can't we?" Coal asked. He liked living around magic and being in the fey realm, but if living in the human realm meant that he would be able to be with Chalcedony, he would do it a thousand times over. He reached out to touch her hand, but she pulled away.

"Too many of my fey would die while Tetrick's mother and Queen Isis fought over Everleaf."

"Why can't you just leave everything to Madoc?" Coal asked, trying to hide his embarrassment at her rejection.

"No male shall rule. You know that. The other queens have only left me alone because it's against the law to rage war against a queenling. Besides, my mother made it clear before she died that my duty would always be to rule and protect Everleaf. I've never had an option, and neither will my oldest daughter. I'm cursed to reign, just as Madoc is cursed to serve."

"Hi," squeaked a small child wearing a pink dress and a tiara. Surprised, Coal and Chalcedony stared at the child, speechless.

"Hi," Chalcedony said, the first to recover.

"Are you a fairy princess?" the girl asked.

Chalcedony laughed nervously. "Why?"

"Because you have pointy ears. I'm a princess, too." The girl tapped her tiara and swung her waist-length jet-black hair from side to side. "I'm not a fairy, though. Are you?"

Chalcedony glanced briefly at Coal.

"What's your name?"

"Elizabeth. I'm six." The girl smiled, showing a large gap where her two front teeth should've been. "Where did you come from?"

"I am from the land of the fey," Chalcedony said with a low mischievous tone.

"Fey like a fairy?" Elizabeth's eyes were wide with joy. "Can I go there with you?"

"Elizabeth!" Someone shouted from across the shop. A woman, an exact copy of Elizabeth, only taller and plumper, walked towards them. Behind her sat a baby strapped in a high chair banging a piece of bread against a plate.

"Momma, look. She's a fairy. See. She has pointy ears," Elizabeth said when the woman reached their table.

"She does not have pointy ears," her mother said with a strained smile before she faced Chalcedony. "I'm so sorry. She says some of the most incredible things sometimes."

Chalcedony said, "That's alright. She's not bothering us."

"Let's go, Lizzy." The woman pulled Elizabeth towards the table where the baby sat.

Chalcedony spun towards Coal. Her eyes glowed with elation. "I've been to the human realm dozens of times. Besides you, I've never met another human who saw through glamour. Never!"

Madoc sat in his office, hunched over his desk, trying to find the source of the pollution in the giants' water supply. He'd gone out himself to track the cause, but had found nothing. If it had only been poisoned once, the giants probably would have ignored it, but it had happened three times. They blamed the dwarves who lived and mined in the mountains upstream. Thankfully, neither the giants nor Madoc proved the dwarves had anything to do with it. The last thing they needed was a war.

A slow, hesitant tap at the door brought Madoc out of his thoughts. "What is it?" he asked, welcoming the distraction.

Bren stepped into Madoc's office. "Sir, I'm checking in from the forest."

Madoc leaned forward in his chair. "I'm listening,"

"They were there," Bren began. "I was hiding as you recommended, but when I saw them in a … questionable position, I had to interrupt and make sure the princess was not being harmed."

"What do you mean questionable position?"

Bren cleared his throat. "They were … they appeared to be kissing."

"It's either they were or they weren't." Madoc suppressed a smile, amused by Bren's obvious discomfort. Bren paused and lifted his head.

"They were kissing, sir."

A slow grin crept across Madoc's face. Well, they finally crossed the line. "What did the princess say when you interrupted them?"

"She was surprised and asked where I had come from."

"Did you tell her I sent you?"

"I told her you had told me to patrol the forest."

"And she believed you?" Madoc asked.

"Yes."

"Good." Few of his guards were so good at lying. "Did you tell anyone else about this?"

"No, sir," Bren said, recoiling as if he'd been insulted. "Of course not."

"Well." Madoc sat back in his chair. "Don't feel like you have to keep it a secret."

Bren grimaced and narrowed his eyes in confusion. Madoc crossed his arms across his chest.

"I want you to spread this rumor of them kissing. It may be a helpful catalyst to get the human out of this realm."

Bren nodded. "Yes, sir. I understand."

"Good. You're dismissed."

After Bren left, Madoc closed his eyes. He tried to predict where this relationship with Chalcedony and Coal would lead. It could only end one way: nowhere. He wanted to kill the boy to ensure that, but he trusted his prophets. They rarely foresaw anything, so when they did, he listened and obeyed. He felt the change in the air. He had no idea what was coming, but he was looking forward to watching it play out.

Chalcedony couldn't stop staring at Elizabeth. The girl reminded her so much of Coal at that age.

"Chalcedony," Coal said.

She turned towards Coal. For a moment, she'd forgotten he'd come with her.

"You okay?" he asked.

"I'm fine." Coal was trying to look comfortable. But she'd known him for too long to be fooled. His shoulders were squared as if he was waiting for someone to start a fight with him. He gripped his mug as if it was the only thing between him and death.

"You don't like it here, do you?" Chalcedony asked.

"No," he answered without hesitation.

"Why?"

"I'm not sure. I was homeless before you found me. Maybe that has something to do with it. When we first arrived, I remembered a woman. I think she was my mother, but then she left me." Coal changed the subject. "What are we going to do about the kiss?"

She rubbed the back of her neck. She could dodge the question again, but he would just keep bringing it up. Besides, he was right. It needed to be addressed. "There is nothing we can do about it. Madoc will kill you if ..." she trailed off. "We have to forget about it." She glanced at the ground, willing the memory of their kiss away. "We're best friends. That's all we can ever be."

"Queen Isis, in the south, has a human mate and no children." He stared at his cup.

"She's a hundred years older than me. No one doubts she's strong enough to fight for her lands. I don't have that luxury."

"Why don't you fight for what you want?" Coal pressed.

She couldn't let herself even think about being with him. The thought felt like a betrayal to her mother and all she'd worked for since birth. "Why did we have to grow up? It was so much simpler when we ran around Legacy all day without—"

"Without wanting to kiss each other in the middle of it," he said with a crooked smile.

"No." She laughed despite herself. "When we were younger, we spent all day together without everyone gossiping."

He sobered suddenly. "Are you going to leave me here?"

"I told you already. I would never do that. Do you want to stay?"

"No, I hate it here," he responded as if she'd accused him of stealing something.

"Don't worry about it." Yes, it would solve everything, but the thought of being without him scared her. Out of the corner of her eye, Chalcedony saw Elizabeth waving goodbye as her mother hustled her out of the door.

"Are you finished?" Chalcedony asked, standing. Coal placed his cup on the table and stood.

"Yes."

"Let's go." Chalcedony hurried out of the shop. Just as they bounded onto the street, Elizabeth and her family turned the corner. Chalcedony walked faster.

"Are we leaving now?" Coal matched Chalcedony's pace.

"Not yet."

"Then, where are we going?"

"You'll see," she answered, but she didn't really know herself. She wanted to talk to the girl again.

As Chalcedony expected, Elizabeth and her family didn't live far from the coffee shop. Humans drove most places, but not if they lived on a college campus. Elizabeth's mother unlocked the door to their apartment and stepped in. Chalcedony followed, waited a few moments, and knocked.

"Why are we here?" Coal asked, with an impatient, accusatory tone.

"Shh."

"No. Why are we here?"

She knocked again, ignoring his burning gaze.

"Oh, hi? Did I forget something at the restaurant?" Elizabeth's mother asked, recognition showing in her eyes.

"Yes," Chalcedony said. "Can we come in?"

"Um." She eyed Chalcedony and Coal. "What do you want?"

Before she lost her nerve, Chalcedony brought the pouch of glamour from under her shirt and blew the powder into the woman's face.

Coal is Available on Amazon, Barnes and Nobles, and Itunes.

ABOUT THE AUTHOR

Constance Burris is on a journey to take over the world through fantasy, horror, and science fiction. Her mission is to spread the love of speculative fiction to the masses. She is a proud card carrying blerd (black nerd), mother, and wife. When she is not writing and spending time with her family, she is working hard as an environmental engineer in Oklahoma City.

www.twitter.com/constanceburris
www.facebook.com/constance.burris
www.constanceburris.com

AUTHOR NOTES

Please help me on my mission to take over the world, and leave a review on Goodreads, Amazon, Barnes and Noble, and Kobo. World domination is impossible without helpful minions, faithful followers, and book reviews.

I absolutely love to talk to readers, so please connect with me through Facebook, Google+, Twitter, or my blog. What do you think about Crazy Jade? Is she bad, or is she just misunderstood? Personally, I feel like she's misunderstood, but I have a soft spot for bad girls.

Made in the USA
Coppell, TX
02 November 2020

40642365R00111